TURT

Elizabeth Laird was born in New Zealand but when she was three the family moved to England. Since then she has travelled to the furthest corners of the world and has encountered all kinds of animals. On one adventure she became lost at night in a Kenyan game reserve, coming a little too close to an angry rhino and narrowly avoiding buffalo and elephants. Her experience of the wild animals of Africa has helped her write the *Wild Things* series.

She is the award-winning author of *Red Sky in the Morning*, *Kiss the Dust*, *Secret Friends* (shortlisted for the 1997 Carnegie Medal) and many other children's novels.

Elizabeth Laird has been helped in her research for *Wild Things* by Kenyan wildlife experts and ordinary country people, whose lives are constantly touched by the animals amongst which they live.

Books available in the Wild Things series

1. Leopard Trail
2. Baboon Rock
3. Elephant Thunder
4. Rhino Fire
5. Red Wolf
6. Zebra Storm
7. Parrot Rescue
8. Turtle Reef

Coming soon

9. Chimp Escape June 2000
10. Lion Pride August 2000

WILD THINGS

TURTLE REEF

Elizabeth Laird

MACMILLAN CHILDREN'S BOOKS

Series consultant: Dr Shirley Strum with the support of Dr David Western, past director of the Kenya Wildlife Service

First published 2000 by Macmillan Children's Books
a division of Macmillan Publishers Limited
25 Eccleston Place, London SW1W 9NF
Basingstoke and Oxford
www.macmillan.co.uk

Associated companies throughout the world

ISBN 0 330 39302 2

1 3 5 7 9 8 6 4 2

A CIP catalogue record for this book is available from the British Library.

Phototypeset by Intype London Ltd
Printed and bound in Great Britain by Mackays of Chatham plc, Kent

For Patriciah, Edwin, Eric and Mike

whose mother, Janet Kaleha, is the warden of Shimoni National Park in Kenya. She took me out in her patrol boat, introduced me to the fishermen in the villages nearby, and shared with me her deep understanding of the coral, the turtles, the shells, the fish, the Indian Ocean, and the people who live beside it.

ACKNOWLEDGEMENTS

Macmillan Children's Books and Elizabeth Laird would also like to send their special thanks to Alan and Kate Riley and all those who belong to the Turtle Watch at Watamu.

It was still barely past the middle of the day and the sun, filtering down through the clear water, cast deep shadows over the coral reef and its undersea world of miniature cliffs and gulches.

In a cleft, the turtle waited. Almost in front of her nose, a shoal of brilliant miniature fish twisted and turned in perfect unison, while a solitary parrotfish, its body a sunburst of pinks and blues, browsed on the coral. It made its progress with leisurely twists of its tail, its bright eyes swivelling in its head as it watched for danger.

The turtle had come in days ago from the deep ocean, feeling a need, an instinct, which had drawn her back to this place through thousands of miles of water, from the other side of the world.

Countless tides had risen and fallen, and she had seen the moon grow and disappear many times since she had last been here. She had been a tiny hatchling then, no bigger than an oyster, and she had struggled out of her egg and tumbled down the beach, away from the nest her mother had made, racing with her crowd of siblings in a mad scramble to the sea. Crabs and gulls had snatched some of the others before they had even reached the water's edge, and rapacious fish had eaten many others in their first few weeks of life. Somehow though, she had survived.

She had still been some way out at sea, swimming with strong strokes towards the familiar reef, when something had almost stopped her. Coming up for air, as she regularly needed to do, she had seen the barnacled keel of a huge ship. She had encountered such things before, in her many years of travelling through the oceans. She had slipped past ferries, tankers, yachts and container ships, escaping as fast as she could from the disturbing thrum of their engines.

This time, though, something strange was in the water. In front of her was what looked like an invisible wall from which hundreds of fish, eels, rays and even a dolphin were struggling to free themselves. The wall lay across her chosen route and she swam towards it, but a few seconds before it could entangle her too, a shark, nosing nearby, alarmed her and she made a sudden dive. When she came up again, the trawler's net was disappearing, hauled into the ship above by clanking machinery that echoed for miles through the ocean, penetrating right down to the sandy bed far below.

Not understanding her narrow escape, she had reached the reef in safety. She had fed there peacefully for days, and at last had found a mate. Now her eggs were ripe. They were ready to be laid, and could not wait any longer. Tonight, when the tide was high, would be the time. She would swim out of the familiar sea, whose dangers she had managed to avoid, and she would make the arduous, perilous journey up the hostile beach to dig her nest, near where she herself had hatched.

There she would lay her eggs.

1

AN UNDERWATER WORLD

Afra climbed over the side of the inflatable boat and clung to it nervously with one hand while she adjusted her goggles and snorkel with the other. Joseph was already floating face down, rising and falling on the low swell, and Afra could see by the stillness of his arms and legs that the underwater world beneath him, the multitude of corals and the shoals of darting fish, was absorbing him completely.

The water of the Indian Ocean was warm, and the sun beating down on Afra's head was very hot, but she realized she was shivering.

I can't be scared, she told herself. I can swim just fine. I won't drown. What's wrong with me? Joseph's enjoying this. Why can't I?

Joseph's uncle Titus, who was keeping the boat steady with one hand on the tiller, looked over the round inflated side down onto her bobbing head.

'What is it, Afra? Is something wrong?'

There was a note of anxiety in his rich African voice.

'Nothing,' she called back up to him hastily.

She gave the goggles one last tweak, clamped the mouthpiece of her snorkel between her teeth and let go of the side of the boat. She swam a few strokes, then gingerly lowered her face into the water. This was the moment she had been dreading. She was afraid of water rushing in round the rubber seal of her goggles, of the salt stinging her eyes and running down her nose, suffocating her.

The seal was good. She found, after one awkward, indrawn gasp, that she could breathe easily through the snorkel with her mouth.

Her confidence grew. The current was pulling her irresistibly towards something that rose like a mass of rocks from the sandy sea floor below. She could see it clearly now. It was a tree – no, a rocky eruption – no, a garden of coral. Joseph was ahead of her. She could see his dark brown legs flicking steadily through the water. He seemed to be beckoning her to come towards him.

She swam up to him. She was right over the coral now. If she was careless and kicked too hard, she risked touching it, and might even break one of the perfect, fragile, rose-tinted scallop-like shapes that lay close under the surface of the sea.

Joseph grasped her arm, then pointed downwards. A shoal of tiny electric blue fish, each one no bigger than a man's thumbnail, was swimming in perfect formation along the wall of coral. Behind them cruised a much larger fish, its plump sides gleaming as its pretty pink and turquoise scales caught the light. The little fish turned at exactly the same moment and darted away out of sight, behind a branching structure of coral.

Afra, suddenly aware that a trickle of water was oozing into her goggles, came up for air and lifted them to let the water run out. She could see the beach not far away, a perfect tropical paradise of white sand fringed with graceful coconut palms.

A tall figure wearing a battered sunhat was walking along by the edge of the water. She could recognize him easily. It was Professor Tovey, her father.

She lifted a hand to wave at him.

'Prof, hey, it's me!' she wanted to shout, but it was too much effort to dislodge the snorkel from her mouth, and anyway, Prof was too far away to hear her.

She watched him turn off the beach and walk up through the low sand dunes towards Mr Mohammed's old-fashioned guest house where they were staying for their holiday. He would be going round to the front and out to the road. She remembered now. He'd said a friend was coming down to the coast, to stay at the big tourist hotel just along the beach. They'd be meeting regularly over the next few days.

Some nerdy old archaeologist, I guess, thought Afra resignedly. He'll have bits of ancient bones in his pockets, and dusty old sandals, and he and Prof will get really boring about dates and stuff.

Prof was out of sight now. Afra settled the goggles back on her face and put her head down into the water again.

She was getting used to the reef now, to the miniature world of light and shade, of darting shapes and brilliant, shifting colours. Its beauty was drawing her in.

A couple of black and white zebra humbug fish, the size of her hand, floated past her face, their round eyes hardly seeming to notice her. Behind them, bigger and more dignified, came an emperor angelfish, its sides a marvel of purple and yellow stripes, its golden fins seeming hardly to move as it steered itself with no visible effort towards a cluster of succulent sponges.

Afra's eyes drifted downwards, following a dazzling parrotfish. What was that down there, that thing, forming a round dark shape on a ledge? Was it just the entrance to a little coral cave?

No, the shape was moving. She could see it more clearly now. A head with a curved beak was sticking out of a huge oval patterned shell, and four delicate flippers were working gently against the water as the big creature rose in an elegant spiral, showing for a moment the creamy skin of its neck before it turned deftly onto its side, and, with a final thrust of its paddle-like flippers, disappeared round the edge of a coral outcrop.

It was a sea turtle.

Afra almost let go of her mouthpiece in her excitement. She looked round for Joseph and signalled to him with vigorous thrusts of her arms, but he was too far away to notice her, and lost, face down, in rapt contemplation of the underwater world.

I've seen a turtle, Afra thought, with deep satisfaction.

They were rare, she knew. She'd seen pictures of them on lists of endangered species. She'd read about their mysterious lives, their thousand-mile journeys across the oceans of the world, their sandy nests on tropical shores.

And I've seen one, she told herself again jubilantly.

She had drifted a little further than she had intended, beyond the coral, and was looking down onto the bare sandy bed of the ocean, four or five metres below her. There were fewer fish here, but something else was down there, something that was moving, a great diamond-shaped body, as broad as her big beach towel. It was flapping along on the bottom, raising spurts of sand, and Afra could see now that it had a long tail that whipped through the water behind it.

A stingray! she thought with a spurt of panic.

She lifted her head out of the water and looked round wildly. The grey inflatable was a good hundred metres away. The current must have swept her further than she'd realized. She let go of the mouthpiece and began to swim as fast as she could, but the current was too strong for her. The small breeze of early afternoon had strengthened now to a blustery wind, churning the water into choppy little waves.

'Hey! Uncle Titus!' she called out.

But Titus didn't hear. An old white motor boat had pulled up alongside the inflatable. Afra could see a ranger in the uniform of the Kenya Wildlife Service at the wheel, and behind the ranger a big woman wearing a white T-shirt, who was talking and laughing with Titus.

'Uncle Titus!' Afra called again, trying to stop her voice sounding shrill with panic. The stingray had scared her badly. She didn't dare look down to see if it was any closer. She wanted only to reach the safety of the boat, but the current seemed to be drawing her further and further away.

Something brushed against her leg.

'Help! Uncle Titus!' she screamed.

At last, Titus heard her. He said something over his shoulder to the woman and turned the boat towards Afra. A moment later he had pulled up alongside her, and was leaning down to haul her out of the water. As she tumbled into the inflatable, Afra saw, with a secret sense of shame, that it was only a piece of seaweed that had touched her leg. It was clinging to her still. She peeled it off and dropped it back into the sea.

'What happened to you?' asked Titus. 'Don't tell me you saw a shark?'

'No. A stingray. It was so huge. Oh, and Titus, you won't believe this. I saw a turtle. It was just the most beautiful thing. It was big, too. Nearly a metre long, I guess.'

The KWS patrol boat had followed the grey inflatable and the woman who had been talking to Titus leaned forward with interest. Her straightened hair had been blown around by the sea breeze, and her dark eyes were alight with enthusiasm.

'You saw a turtle?'

She had to shout above the noise of the two engines.

'Yes!' Afra yelled back. 'A big one.'

'Did you see what kind it was?'

The woman was steadying herself with one hand as the boat rocked on the increasingly choppy water.

'I don't know,' Afra said. 'Is there more than one kind?'

The woman grabbed hold of the side of the launch as it rolled on the swell. She looked large and maternal, almost incongruous here out at sea.

'Yes,' she said. 'There are five on this coast. They're all rare, all very special. You were so lucky to see one today. I hope it was a female. Maybe she's coming in to lay.'

'To lay?' Afra wasn't sure if she'd heard right above the noise of the engine.

'To make a nest in the sand and lay her eggs. Turtles struggle so much to give birth! They are sea creatures, made for swimming, but they have to pull themselves right up the beach, and dig out a pit in the sand.' She gave Afra a wink and a smile. 'The females, they're always the ones who have a hard time.'

Afra tried to imagine the graceful creature she had seen working its way overland on its fragile flippers, and failed. She was just about to ask another question when a spluttering noise came from behind her. She turned to see Joseph's head appear above the side of the inflatable. He was looking at his uncle reproachfully.

'I have been calling you to come and get me, but you didn't hear. The current is so strong! I was afraid I would end up in Australia.'

The woman on the patrol boat laughed, her generously sized body rocking gently.

'Who's this, Titus? I didn't know you had a son.'

'He's my nephew, Joseph,' said Titus, putting a hand under Joseph's shoulder to heave him into the boat. 'And this is his friend, his foster-sister, Afra. Afra and Joseph, this is Grace Otieno, the only woman warden of a game park in the whole of Kenya.'

Joseph wrinkled his nose, puzzled.

'A game park? There is no game park here.'

Grace raised her eyebrows comically.

'No game park? You are sitting in it right now. My game park is under the sea.'

'But there aren't any animals for you to protect,' objected Joseph.

'No animals?' Grace's eyebrows were now so high they nearly disappeared under her wild wisps of hair. 'Your friend has just seen a turtle, for one thing. And what about the fish you have seen, and the shells and the corals? Don't they need protecting too?'

'Turtles, of course,' said Afra doubtfully, 'but the coral's just sort of like rock, isn't it?'

Grace rolled her eyes at Titus.

'Titus, haven't you taught these kids anything? Coral is alive, like a plant, and it's rare and beautiful and precious. Everyone wants a piece of it. They take it and take it, more and more, to put in their cabinets and make their necklaces and earrings and bracelets, and if I wasn't here to guard it there would soon be nothing left.'

'Wow.' Afra was wrapping a towel round herself, feeling suddenly a little chilly, in spite of the sun. 'I didn't know. I had no idea that the coral needed protecting.'

'Well, it does,' said Grace. 'Anytime you feel

like buying a coral necklace, just buy a nice little glass one instead.'

The wind was still rising and the ranger of the patrol boat was finding it hard to keep it alongside the little inflatable. He said something to Grace in Swahili.

'*Twende, endelea*,' she called back to him. 'OK, let's go.' Then she swept the occupants of the inflatable with her wide warm smile.

'Come and see me, you kids,' she said. 'I'll tell you all about my reef. And I'd like to hear about the turtle you saw, Afra. My office is just there, see? That little white building above the jetty, by that clump of coconut trees.'

Afra nodded and smiled back. It was impossible not to smile at Grace Otieno. There was something about her broad kindly face and sturdy strong body that made you like her at once, and told you that you could rely on her too.

She turned her head to look where Grace was pointing. The boats had drifted further in towards the beach now. Afra had been sitting on the bottom of the inflatable, her towel wrapped round her, but now she let it fall and rose to her knees. She could see her father again. He must have gone to meet his friend and they'd come back together. But his friend wasn't a musty old professor of archaeology. It was a tall young woman dressed in a loose crimson dress, and even from here Afra could see that her hair was a smooth burnished blonde.

The pair turned to look out towards the boats, and Afra stiffened.

Her father was holding the strange woman's hand.

2

A LITTLE BOX

It seemed a lifetime before Titus cut the engine of the inflatable and jumped out into the shallow water to pull it up onto the white sand. Afra's stomach was churning.

She can't be a girlfriend! Prof's never *had a girlfriend, ever, since my mother died. He only ever loved her. He still does. He must!*

She didn't dare look at Joseph, who had shot one shocked glance at the couple on the beach and looked away again.

It's a long-lost cousin, that's why he's holding her hand, or – or the woman's blind or something, and he's just helping her along, Afra told herself desperately, but as soon as she'd scrambled out of the boat, and was standing looking up at her father, she knew her worst fears had been realized. Prof wasn't holding the woman's hand any more, but he had an anxious, guilty, soft expression on his face that made Afra want to hit him.

Prof cleared his throat.

'Afra,' he said, with a horrible false cheerfulness. 'This, is – ah – a very good friend of mine. Minette.'

The woman, whose creamy fair skin was tanned to a light gold, and whose eyes were a subtle greeny-blue, parted her red lips in a smile intended to dazzle.

'Hello, Afra,' she said.

Her voice was high and light, and she spoke with a slight French accent.

Afra grunted. She couldn't bring herself to say hello back.

'Minette's staying at the Ocean View Hotel, just along the breach,' Prof said, with grating breeziness. 'She'll be around for the next two weeks. It'll give you two a chance to get to know each other.'

Afra's head was spinning with shock.

This is a nightmare. It's not happening, she told herself.

Before she knew what she was doing, she had whirled round on her feet and was racing away along the beach.

'Afra,' Prof called out after her, without conviction, and she ran faster, desperate to get away.

Footsteps thundered after her. She put on a spurt, running as fast as she could, but the person behind was too fast for her. She felt a hand clutch her arm and shook it off.

'Afra, it's only me,' Joseph said.

She stopped, winded and disappointed, her breath coming in shuddering pants.

'Leave me alone.'

'I brought your towel,' said Joseph. 'You dropped it.'

He held it out to her, but she thrust his outstretched hand away.

'I don't want it.'

'I know.' He shook his head, as if clearing his mind. 'I just wanted an excuse to get away from them too.'

She heard shock and sympathy in his voice.

'I don't *believe* it,' she burst out. 'You saw them. You heard him! She's like a – she's like his girlfriend or something. They were holding hands!'

'I know. It was awful. Who is she?'

She had wanted him to tell her she was wrong, that she'd been imagining things, and the fact that he didn't filled her with sudden rage.

'How should I know? I never saw her before in my life! She's just a – a horrible – I don't know – a thief. Yes, a thief! She's trying to steal my father!'

Joseph frowned.

'You can't steal a person, Afra,' he said reasonably. 'I mean, if Prof wants to be with her, if he's fallen in love with her—'

'*Don't*! Don't *say* that!' she was beginning to feel hysterical.

'No, but I mean, if he likes her, or something, it's normal. He has been alone now since you were born. More than twelve years! It is a very long time for a man. For anyone.'

'But he loved my mother!' A sob rose in Afra's throat. 'She was the love of his life! And she was an Ethiopian! How could he possibly even look, for one second, at that – that blonde Barbie doll!'

Joseph pursed his lips.

'She's very pretty.'

'*Pretty*?' Afra was feeling sick. 'And anyway, why didn't he tell me if he was planning to get himself a girlfriend or something? I have the right to know, don't I? I'm his daughter, for pete's sake, aren't I?'

'Maybe he didn't know. Maybe he only just met her, you know, last week, when he was working on that dig over at Gedi.'

'Gedi!' Afra spat the word out with loathing. Gedi was an ancient ruined city, half-hidden in the thick forest further up the coast. Prof had been working there half of last term, leaving her alone at home in Nairobi with Joseph and her foster-mother, Sarah. She had felt jealous enough of the place that had taken her father away from home and absorbed his whole attention for weeks and weeks, but she'd had no idea that another, much greater threat would creep out of those sinister ruins to wreck her peace and happiness.

Joseph was looking back along the beach. Prof and Minette had helped Titus drag the inflatable up the beach and upend it beyond the high watermark. Now they were standing together, deep in conversation.

'Uncle Titus is saying goodbye, I think,' Joseph said. 'He is returning today to Nairobi. We must go and say goodbye to him, Afra.'

She wanted to shake her head and refuse, to go on running down the beach and never come back. She hated the thought of walking back tamely, into the orbit of Minette, but reluctantly she nodded. Titus had been great these last few days. She had to thank him, at the very least, for taking them out snorkelling today.

Joseph had already set off, back along the beach. Afra began to trail after him, then, afraid of looking childish, she ran to catch him up, and they were walking side by side when they reached the group of adults.

Prof took one quick look at her, then bit his lip and dropped his eyes. Minette nervously smoothed her already perfect hair, which was clipped back by a slide at the nape of her neck. Titus smiled warmly at Afra.

'I have been telling your father, Afra, how you saw a turtle and a stingray.'

'Did you really?' Minette said too enthusiastically. 'How wonderful!'

Afra ignored her.

'Thank you very much, Uncle Titus,' she said formally, 'for taking us out today.' Her voice was tight with misery.

'That's OK.' He had put his towel and his bundle of dry clothes down on the sand, and now he bent to pick them up. 'It's always fun going around with you kids. I'm sorry I have to go back. But your father's here now. You'll have a great time, all of you. Joseph, come up to the house with me. I need some help to take my bag to the bus stop.'

He bounded off up the low sand dune with Joseph at his heels. Joseph turned and gave Afra a last look, compressing his lips sympathetically, then he was gone, and she was alone with Prof and Minette.

Minette looked from one to the other and gave a little high-pitched laugh.

'I'll see you both later,' she said. 'Afra, Richard says he'll bring you to dinner with me at the hotel tonight. They do a fabulous buffet there. You'll love it.'

Afra, wincing as she heard her father's first name on Minette's lips, grimaced but said nothing.

'Well then,' Minette said, after a little pause. 'Till this evening.'

She turned and went off, her bare feet marking the perfect white sand, her elegant sandals dangling from one hand.

Prof tried to put his arm round Afra's shoulders.

'Honey,' he began.

'Don't – touch – me,' she hissed.

He dropped his arm and dug his hands into his pockets.

'Look, I tried to tell you. I said I'd be seeing a friend down here, remember? I met Minette at Gedi. She was buying stuff from the crafts people near there, for her store. She runs a kind of craft shop in Nairobi.'

'She lives in Nairobi? You're going to go on seeing her when we get home?'

Despair was in Afra's voice.

Prof hesitated.

'I don't know. I hope so.' He cleared his throat. 'Afra, I like Minette. She's a very nice person, a very special person. We have a lot in common. She makes me laugh.'

'And I don't, I suppose?'

'Of course you do!' He sounded annoyed. 'Anyway, Minette has nothing to do with what happens between you and me. I'm your daddy. You're my girl. That will never change. But I guess I need just a little more in my life sometimes.'

'Oh you do? And what about her – I mean, what about my mother?' Afra was battling to keep the tears out of her voice.

'Your mother died, sweetheart. I loved her. You know that. I'll never love anyone that way again. But it's been a long time. I guess I'm allowed to see someone else, after nearly thirteen years. You could try to like Minette you know. She so much wants to get along with you, to be friends, and—'

'Oh, I'm sure she does!' Afra laughed jeeringly. 'She wants to get hold of you, and she knows what she has to do. She knows she has to be all sweet and nice as pie with me. It's pathetic. And if you think I'm coming with you to that stupid hotel tonight, leaving Joseph here on his own—'

'Joseph's invited too, of course,' Prof said quickly. 'Didn't she say?'

'No. She did not say.'

'Afra, honey.' Prof tried putting his hand on her shoulder again. This time, she didn't pull away. 'I want you to try, OK? I'm asking you to do this. I don't know Minette very well yet. Nothing has been decided between us. We only met three weeks ago. All I want is to get to know her a little better, for us both to get to know her.'

She said nothing.

'Oh yes, I forgot.' He put his hand in the breast pocket of his bush shirt and pulled out a little package wrapped in tissue paper. 'Minette bought a present for you. She asked me to give it to you.'

He held the package out. Afra wanted to smack his hand away, but unwillingly she let him drop the package into her palm. She unfolded the tissue paper. On it lay a little flat box, no more than four centimetres square. She picked it up and examined it. It was gleaming, polished, a rich brown colour shot through with streaks of golden yellow.

'It's made of turtle shell!' she cried.

As if it were scorching hot, she dropped the little box on the sand. Images of the lovely turtle she had seen, swimming wild and free of fear around the coral reef, flashed through her mind.

'Prof, it's *disgusting*!' she cried. 'It's – it's murder! Doesn't she know, is she so stupid she doesn't even *know* that you must never buy anything made of turtle shell? Doesn't she *care* about the turtles? Does she want to make them extinct? I wouldn't take this thing, I wouldn't even *touch* it, if you gave me a million dollars!'

She could hold back her tears no longer. Her cheeks streaming, she ran up the beach towards the guest house, leaving her father standing alone, the little box lying in the sand at his feet.

3

HUSSEIN

Lunch was a difficult meal for everyone. Mr Mohammed, the owner of the guest house, was his usual ebullient self, serving up a wonderful concoction of chicken with a spicy coconut sauce, but Afra, Joseph and Prof ate in silence.

The dining room of the guest house was no more than a shelter, open on two sides to the garden and on one side to the sea. Afra had always loved sitting here. She had revelled in the bright flowers of the scarlet hibiscus and purple bougainvillea, with the turquoise sea behind them. Today, though, the colours looked garish and jarring, and Mr Mohammed's cheerfulness grated on her nerves so much she wanted to say something rude to him.

Prof ate steadily through his lunch, looking at Afra from time to time with a kind of puzzled sympathy that made her squirm. Joseph tried once or twice to talk, describing the coral and fishes he'd seen on the reef that morning, but the atmosphere was too heavy, and he soon gave up.

Afra ate no more than a couple of mouthfuls. Everything tasted horrible today, and there was a big lump in her throat that no swallowing could dislodge. As soon as she could, she pushed her plate away.

'I'm going to the beach,' she said. 'Are you coming, Joseph?'

Joseph quickly scooped up the last mouthful of rice and chicken, and washed it down with a long draught of passion fruit juice. Then he looked up enquiringly at Prof.

'Yes, yes, go on, you two,' said Prof, looking relieved. 'You have all afternoon. Minette doesn't expect us till seven.'

Afra waited until she and Joseph had jumped down off the dunes and were back on the sandy beach.

'Minette doesn't expect us till seven,' she said at last, in a mocking, singsong voice. 'Well, if she thinks I'm going to her dumb hotel, to eat her poisonous buffet, she can go jump in the sea. I'd choke. I'd throw up. Bits would fall off me. I'm not going anywhere near her or her place. Ever.'

Joseph shrugged his shoulders.

'You will be sorry to miss the meringues,' he said. 'Uncle Titus told me they're wonderful at the hotel. He went to dinner there last year. I'll bring one home for you.'

'Joseph!' They had been walking along the high tideline, stepping over piles of seaweed, but Afra stopped dead in her tracks and glared at him.

'You wouldn't! You couldn't go without me! It would – you would betray me!'

He raised his eyebrows.

'Afra, you are so stupid sometimes. What good will it do if we don't go? Do you want to leave them alone together? My grandfather used to tell me that when he was young, and the men of his tribe were fighting with another tribe, they would never retreat. Never! They would go to face their enemies, and see how strong their enemies were. Then they could plan how to defeat them.'

Afra digested this in silence.

'You should put your new dress on tonight,' Joseph went on, 'and smile, and say nice things. Then you can find out what's going on, and what you have to do.'

A revolted look had settled on Afra's face.

'Put on my new dress? Are you kidding? It's pink! It has frills! It makes me look like Pollyanna!'

'It doesn't.' Joseph was offended, although he had never heard of Pollyanna. 'Mama bought it for you. She said it was the prettiest dress in the shop.'

Afra kicked at a stone.

'Anyway, it makes you look like a girl,' Joseph said defensively. 'That is a change. Sometimes I forget you are a girl at all.' He put up an arm to wipe his dripping forehead with his sleeve. 'How far are we going to walk? It's so hot! No one except you goes out in the sun at this time of day. It's crazy.'

As she walked, Afra was digging her feet into the sand as if she wanted to bruise her toes.

'I don't care how far we walk or what we do.'

Joseph shaded his eyes with his hand.

'Look, over there,' he said. 'Just past that big rock. I went there yesterday with Uncle Titus. There are some nice trees behind it, on the far side. It will be shady there. And the sea comes up nearly as far as the trees. I saw some old boats around there yesterday. We can take a look at them.'

Even to his own ears, it didn't sound like a very interesting plan. Afra didn't answer. Joseph waited for a moment, then, for want of anything better to do, he set off along the beach at a brisker pace. Afra followed him listlessly.

They rounded the big rock and stopped. A group of men were pulling three dugout canoes up out of the water. They looked up at Joseph and Afra and called '*Jambo*! *Salaam*!' in friendly greeting.

A boy, who looked about twelve years old although he was quite small, was working with them. He stared at Joseph and Afra curiously, then one of the men said something to him in a language neither Joseph nor Afra could understand. The boy reached into the canoe nearest to him for a basket, and came towards them, smiling shyly.

'You have come to buy our fish?' he said in Swahili.

Joseph shook his head.

'No. We're staying at Mr Mohammed's place. He does all our food.'

'Oh.' The boy looked disappointed. 'I will show you, anyway.'

He held out the basket and Afra and Joseph looked down into it. Three plump parrotfish lay in it, their gills still gently pulsating, their eyes round and staring, their iridescent pink and blue scales sparkling in the sun. In spite of herself, Afra was intrigued. She looked down at the fish, then stared curiously at the boy.

'Do you always go out fishing? Don't you go to school?'

The boy nodded.

'Yes, sometimes I go. I like to go. But it is the holiday time now. My father is sick today and my uncle, he sent for me to go with him. If I go out and fish with my uncle, he gives me some to take home to my mother. If I don't go, what is there for us to eat? My brothers and sisters will be hungry.'

'Hussein!' one of the men called out. 'Come on! Help us with the nets!'

The boy ran back to the boats. He lifted up a big bundle of green mesh netting. It was an unwieldy burden. A section of it caught on a stone as he dragged it up the beach. Hussein pulled at it.

'Watch out!' the oldest man shouted angrily to him. 'You'll tear the net.'

Afra dashed forward, bent down and released the net from the stone.

'Thank you,' Hussein said softly. 'My uncle, he is very strict. If the net is torn he will punish me.'

Afra had picked up the fish basket and was carrying it up the beach after him.

'Do you live here?' she said, peering curiously up through a fringe of trees at a cluster of square coral-rock houses, thatched with coconut palms.

'Yes. This is my village. Do you want to come to my house? I can give you some coconut milk to drink.'

Joseph nodded enthusiastically. Afra laughed.

'Joseph loves coconut milk. I like it too. It's so hot here. We're really thirsty.'

'Hot?' Hussein looked puzzled. 'It's always like this.'

'It's not in Nairobi, where we come from,' said Joseph. 'It's really cold sometimes.'

The oldest fisherman called out something to Hussein and jerked his head.

'He says I can stop work now,' Hussein said, looking delighted. 'Eh, I am glad to rest. It is very hard, on the boats, putting out the nets and fish traps and taking them in. And the fishing is bad. We have been working all morning, and there is only this much to bring home. My mother will be disappointed again. My dad says, when he was young, they filled their baskets every day, twice even. They caught big fish then, crayfish, snapper, turtles—'

Afra's head came up sharply.

'Turtles? They caught turtles?'

'Yes. The meat was good. And turtle oil is like a medicine, for kids with asthma, you know?'

Afra was frowning fiercely.

'But the turtles are so beautiful! And they're so rare! No one should kill turtles.'

Hussein nodded.

'We know that now, not to kill them any more, because there are not enough. We leave the nests too. Before, we used to eat the eggs.'

Afra looked first disgusted, then relieved.

'That's good, anyway, that you don't eat them any more. Maybe now you're not fishing for them, they'll have a chance to recover and sort of multiply again.'

'Recover? Multiply?' Hussein snorted. 'Nothing can recover here! Everything is so bad. It is not us, the local fishermen, with our little nets, and our canoes, who take all the fish. It's the trawlers! The big boats. Just out there, just beyond the game park, outside the coral reefs, they're waiting. They come from everywhere, from Europe and the Far East, and their nets pick up every single thing out of the sea. Like brooms, they sweep it clean! Everything! Most of the things they catch they don't even want. They throw them back in the water again.'

'Well,' Joseph said pacifically, 'at least they return them to the sea.'

'Yes, but they are dead! Everything is already dead!' cried Hussein.

'You mean,' Afra said indignantly, 'they kill turtles and things when they don't even want them?'

'Yes, of course. They just pick out whatever fish they want, and dump the rest, which has already died, and go back to Europe and the Far East, with all our prawns and our tuna fish. And we have nothing, nothing left to eat.'

'That's all wrong,' burst out Joseph. 'The fish around here should be for the local fishermen.'

'At least there's the park,' said Afra. 'And your reserve round the edge of it. That's protected, isn't it? Grace Otieno told us. No one else is allowed to fish there.'

They had reached the first of the houses now, and sat down gratefully on an old bench under a shady cashew nut tree. Hussein was shaking his head.

'You think the marine park is safe? I'm telling you, it is not safe! The trawlers are not our only enemies. The dynamiters, they are the ones we fear the most.'

'Dynamiters?' Afra and Joseph said together.

'Yes.' In spite of his anger, Hussein smiled at their surprise. 'The fishermen from the south, they are even poorer than we are here. The trawlers took all their fish years ago. Now they sail up to our reserve, in their outrigger canoes, and they throw dynamite into our water. It goes off – boum, boum! – and all the fish, all the sea creatures, all the coral, are killed, like that, dead, at once. These dynamiters, they quickly collect all the fish that have floated onto the surface of the sea, and they escape back again to the south. Oh!' Hussein's face was suffused with anger. 'If I catch any of those guys I'll – I'll blow them out of the water myself! They're thieves! Wreckers! Pirates!'

No one said anything for a moment. Horrible pictures were forming and dissolving in Afra's head: her lovely turtle caught in a net, bundled in with thousands of other sea creatures, dying, crushed and mangled, tossed casually over the side of a boat by careless men. Or, even worse, her turtle, swimming unconcernedly, at peace with the world, and suddenly a shadow appearing overhead, and something falling into the water, and a terrifying explosion . . .

'We've got to *do* something!' she said, jumping to her feet and nearly knocking out of Joseph's hand the coconut brimming with sweet cloudy milk that Hussein had just handed to him.

'What?' said Joseph, looking up at her. 'What can we do?'

She subsided slowly onto the bench again.

'I don't know.'

She thought savagely of the turtle shell box Minette had tried to give her.

'People don't realize, they just don't know what's happening!' she said passionately. 'We could tell them. Tell . . .'

Her voice trailed away.

A sudden deep faint booming sounded in the distance. Hussein leaped to his feet, and began to run down to the shore.

'The dynamiters!' he yelled. 'They're back!'

4

DYNAMITE!

The fishermen had heard the explosions too. They were running back down the beach to their outrigger canoes, shouting to each other.

Hussein had reached his uncle's boat first and was already pushing it out into the water. Afra and Joseph ran up to help him. Hussein's uncle and another man climbed into the boat and pushed off with their feet. Hussein tried to get in after them.

'No!' shouted Hussein's uncle. 'It's too dangerous. Stay here!'

Already, three outrigger canoes had taken to the water. Their owners were poling them energetically through the shallows with their long punting poles, while the crews set up the small triangular sails on the low masts.

'Uncle! You've left your paddle behind!' Hussein shouted, and he picked the paddle up and began to splash out towards the canoes through the waist-high water. His uncle stopped poling and waited for him. Then, as Afra and Joseph watched, there was a brief argument and

Hussein climbed into the dugout. His uncle had obviously relented.

'What are we going to do?' said Afra helplessly. 'If we have to wait around here and do nothing, I'll go crazy. I'll—'

Joseph was already striding off back along the beach.

'Where are you going?' she called out after him.

'To tell Grace Otieno,' Joseph said over his shoulder. 'She's got the KWS power boat.'

Afra ran after him, clapped him on the shoulder and overtook him.

'Genius,' she yelled. 'I'll race you!'

They arrived at the KWS compound lathered with sweat and out of breath. They ran in through the gates and hesitated. Smartly painted little buildings dotted the compound, which was shaded by old mango trees. One building looked more important than the rest. They ran up to it and burst in through the door.

Grace Otieno was sitting at her desk behind a pile of papers, writing busily. She looked up and frowned.

'Please,' panted Joseph. 'I am sorry to bother you, but—' He had no breath to continue.

A look of concern had replaced Grace's frown.

'What's the matter? Are you hurt? Has there been an accident?'

'No!' Afra was gasping for breath too. 'There

were some explosions out at sea. Hussein said it was dynamite.'

'What? Was that the sound of dynamite? I thought it was a truck backfiring.' Grace was up out of her chair and halfway to the door at once. 'Abel! Massoud! Quick!' she called out. 'Get the boat! The dynamiters are back!'

Two rangers in khaki camouflage uniforms, who had been sitting in the shade of a tree, jumped up and ran to the steps at the side of the compound that led directly down to a little jetty. Grace ran after them with Afra and Joseph at her heels. She climbed on board the old white motor boat, but waved the children back.

'I'm sorry. You can't come with me. It can be nasty. These people, they have explosives. They're not afraid to use them.'

Abel had already cast off, and the boat roared away from the little jetty, Massoud at the wheel.

Afra watched it go, feeling helpless and frustrated.

'Now what?' Joseph said.

'Now nothing,' she said gloomily.

The excitement of the last half hour had driven her troubles out of her mind, but they came crowding back to her again.

Prof's in love! she thought, and in spite of herself her lip trembled.

Joseph was looking at her warily.

'We could go up the hill, above the big rock,'

he said. 'There's a kind of lookout point up there. We might be able to see something.'

'OK, let's go,' she said gratefully.

It wasn't a hill exactly, more a low rise, but when the two of them had run up it, through the light undergrowth, they were out of breath again. They sank down onto a piece of flat rock and looked out to sea.

'I can't see anything,' Afra said, her eyes dazzled by the sun.

'Nor can – wait, yes! Over there!' Joseph was shading his eyes with one hand and pointing with the other. 'Three outriggers, our three, I think, and going quite fast. There goes the patrol boat too. Look, it's really moving now!'

Afra screwed her eyes up. She could see them now, the three little canoes with their sails and outrigging, and the white motor boat that had already left them behind. She could see something else, too. Beyond the patrol boat was a larger vessel, too far away to see properly. It had a long dark hull and some kind of sail. It was moving rapidly away.

She shivered.

'What if they're armed? What if they have guns?'

'They won't have any guns. They're too poor.' Joseph shook his head decisively, though his voice was doubtful. 'But even if they don't have guns, they still have dynamite. That's bad enough. If they throw a stick of dynamite into one of those little outriggers . . .'

He stopped. Afra narrowed her eyes again, and stared fiercely out to sea. Some kind of struggle was going on out there, a battle for the reef. She wanted desperately to be out on the water herself, fighting alongside the local fishermen, striking a blow for the turtles.

'It's no good, I can't see what's happening. They're too far away,' she said at last. 'We might as well go back down.'

Slowly, they walked back down the hill and turned in again through the entrance to the KWS compound. They sat on the veranda outside Grace's office. The door was shut and locked now. The caretaker must have come round after Grace had rushed away.

Afra stood up, unable to sit idly for another moment, and looked in through the window of Grace's office. Some kind of chart was pinned to the wall opposite the window. She could see at once that it was a map of the shoreline. She peered at it, wishing she could make it out more clearly, and managed to decipher the words 'Turtle Nesting Sites'.

'Joseph, look at this,' she said. 'There are turtle nests around here. They're marked on this map. And they've got dates beside them. That's weird. The dates are in the future. Look, that one, near the hotel, that's the day after tomorrow, and the one at the end is three weeks from now.'

Joseph joined her at the window.

'Maybe the dates are for when the eggs are due to hatch,' he said doubtfully.

'Of course! That's it! So the turtles have been up to lay already. That one I saw this morning, maybe she was on her way back to the ocean, not coming in to land.'

She was disappointed. She'd half hoped that she might see her turtle again, at night, maybe, if she came in to lay.

The put-put of a boat's engine came from below the steps.

'They're back!' cried Afra. 'Come on!'

They raced down to the jetty. The patrol boat was nearly alongside it already, and the three outrigger canoes were in the distance, coming in slowly under sail.

'What happened?' Afra called out to Grace, who was standing beside Massoud at the wheel. 'Did you catch them?'

The boat bobbed gently up to the jetty and Grace stepped out.

'No, they got away. They had a good start, and we didn't have enough petrol for a long chase.' She began to plod up the steps towards her office again. 'It was a sad sight out there. The dynamiters had already netted up quite a load of fish, but the rest were just floating on the surface –

fish, eels, sponges, all quite dead. And if you looked down below the surface of the sea you could see very big black scars where the coral has been destroyed. Where it has been blown to pieces!'

Afra clenched her fists with fury.

'It's – it's wicked! If I caught those guys—'

Grace looked tired. She set off up the steps.

'Oh Afra, those dynamiters are not our worst enemies. They are victims too. They were fishermen, like the men here, peacefully living from their own stretch of ocean near their own shore, before the foreign trawlers came and took all their fish away from them. They are trying to survive, by fair means or foul. They are trying to feed their families.'

'Yes, but the destruction! It's so – so crazy!' Afra was almost dancing with rage.

'Yes, it's crazy.' Grace put a hand on her side. The steep walk up from the sea had winded her. 'But we are trying to stop them. The best thing would be for them to make another marine park off their coast, off the coast of Tanzania, like the park we have here off our Kenyan coast.'

Joseph looked puzzled.

'Why? No one's allowed to fish in a marine park, are they? That would only make things worse.'

'No, it would make things better.' Grace was unlocking the door of her office now. 'If you make a marine park, and keep that whole area free of fishing, the reef has a chance to recover. It recovers quite quickly, too. There'd be a safe place for the fish to spawn. Then, all around the park, you make a reserve, like the one we have here, where only the local fishermen have the right to fish. Their nets are small, and their traps are quite harmless to most species. They catch the few fish they need to live on around the edges of the park, in their own reserve, but they leave plenty behind to go on breeding. And they make extra money by taking visitors out to see the reef in their boats.'

Afra nodded.

'That's a good idea. Will they do it down there, do you think?'

'Maybe.' Grace sat down wearily at her desk. She pulled a packet of biscuits out of her drawer, offered them to Afra and Joseph, and began to munch one herself. 'It's part of my job to persuade them – and in the meantime to keep the dynamiters away.'

She picked up her pen.

She's tired and busy, thought Afra. She wants us to go away.

'Sorry,' Afra said, 'but I just wanted to know about the map on your wall – the turtle nest sites. Are they there now, those nests, I mean?'

Grace looked up, her face more cheerful.

'Yes, isn't it good? We have three nests just now. At one time, of course, there used to be many dozens of them along here, before so many turtles were slaughtered, but at least we have three. We're guarding them very carefully, I can tell you.'

'Thanks,' said Joseph, tugging at Afra's T-shirt. 'We'll go now. Sorry to disturb you.'

She smiled.

'You haven't disturbed me. You did a good job. You reported the dynamiters. I should be thanking you.'

Afra followed Joseph out of the office.

'Did you hear that?' she barked, storming down the path. 'The turtles have been slaughtered! There are hardly any left! And Miss Barbie Airhead Thinks-she's-so-cool Fashion Freak is so dumb she buys a box made out of turtle shell! And she thinks that I – *I* would be impressed! Well, I've seen that dame coming, and believe me, Joseph, I am going to see her go!'

5

A GASH OF LIPSTICK

For the rest of the afternoon, Afra was in a turmoil of indecision.

'If I go to her horrible buffet tonight, Prof will think I'm kind of agreeing to her,' she said to Joseph.

'If you don't, she will have won the first battle,' answered Joseph.

He was clearly bored with the subject, and didn't want to talk about it any more. Afra gave up. She went to her room, knelt down and began to riffle through the clothes in her suitcase.

The hated pink dress, which Sarah had made her pack 'just in case', as she always said, was bundled into a corner and badly crumpled. Afra held it up and looked at it.

Why don't I just wear it? she asked herself grimly. I'll look such a total disaster Prof will be ashamed to be seen out with me, and he'll just have to turn right around and bring me back here.

But the idea of being seen in public in the dress was too embarrassing even to imagine. She dropped it again and looked through her other clothes. There were two or three pairs of shorts, a few T-shirts, her favourite old jeans and a couple of sunhats.

That's it, she thought, rocking back on her heels with a mixture of satisfaction and anxiety. I can't go. I don't have anything to wear.

Joseph's words were nagging at her though. She bent forward and looked through the suitcase again. Yes, that was better. Rolled up at the back, behind a tangle of pyjamas and underwear, was a short, tight fitting black skirt and a white shirt with a kind of satiny look to it. She had packed them, after all. They were, she thought, the smartest clothes she possessed. Sarah disapproved of them. She thought they were skimpy and showed too much. Afra remembered now that she'd slipped them into the case without Sarah noticing, 'just in case', as she told herself, with a wry smile.

She took off her shorts and old top, shook out the skirt and blouse, and tried them on.

My hair's a mess, she thought, looking at herself in the mirror with disgust, and I don't have any nice shoes, or jewellery, or anything.

The thought of Minette, with her perfectly smooth blonde hair, her richly coloured dress, and the elegant sandals dangling from her manicured hand curdled Afra's stomach, and she plumped herself down on her bed, feeling tears prick her eyelids again.

'Afra, are you there?' Joseph was at the door.

'No, go away. I'm busy.'

'Are you going tonight, or aren't you?'

She hadn't known either, but she suddenly made up her mind.

'I'm going.' She felt her face tense up as she spoke. 'I'm trying to decide what to wear. Come in and help me.'

Joseph opened the door, came in and looked at her in dismay.

'I don't know about clothes,' he said.

'Yes you do.'

She tucked the tails of the blouse into her skirt and turned slowly round in front of him.

'It's OK,' he said unwillingly. 'It doesn't look like you. You usually just wear your old shorts.'

'I know.' She sighed impatiently, looking at herself in the mirror. 'I just wish I had something to go round my neck. Beads or something.'

'Beads?' Joseph had been examining his own torn and dirty fingernails, but now he looked up at her. 'I've got some beads, the ones the Maasai warriors at Ol Tupesi gave me. I brought them because Tom said if we went shopping he wanted me get some exactly the same for him.'

Afra stared at him, mystified. She couldn't imagine Tom, their best friend in Nairobi, wearing strings of red and blue beads.

'Tom?' she said. 'He wants beads?'

'Oh, not for him. For his mum. It's her birthday soon. Anyway, I've got mine here. Do you want to borrow them or not?'

'Do I – yes. I guess so. Yes.'

She was frowning at herself in the mirror again. The bright strips of Maasai beads might look good. Sort of striking and different.

Suddenly she wanted Joseph to bring her the beads and go. She wanted to try things out with her hair. She had brought her new spongebag with her, that Aunt Tidey had sent her from America. It contained, she now remembered, a little make-up kit. She hadn't bothered to look at it yet, but this might be the moment to try some of the stuff out. She could go for the sophisticated look, show Blondie that she wasn't just a silly kid who could be swatted out of the way, like some bothersome insect or something.

'Thanks, Joseph,' she said. 'Can you get me the beads now?'

Joseph went off. He came back a moment later and dumped them on the bed. He seemed to want to stay and talk, but Afra said nothing, and he took the hint and went away.

At ten to seven, Prof knocked tentatively on Afra's door.

'Ready, honey?' he called out. 'It's time to go.'

She opened the door and stood, with one hand on her hip, looking at him defiantly. Prof stepped back and blinked.

A heavy frown was settling on his face.

'What *are* you wearing?' he said.

Her skin was prickling with disappointment

and embarrassment, but she wasn't going to let him see it.

'I'm wearing a shirt,' she said, with a sigh of exaggerated patience. 'A skirt. Some beads. Two sandals. My pantyhose—'

'That's enough!' His eyes snapped angrily. 'Don't you have a dress or something?'

'Yes, I have a dress.' She wanted to burst into tears. 'And no, I'm not, repeat *not* going to wear it.'

He looked at his watch.

'We're late already. Just wipe that stuff off your face.'

'What stuff?' She wanted to slam the door in his face and tell him to go out on his date alone, but she was determined, now, not to leave him and Minette alone.

'That – whatever it is. Lipstick. And the stuff on your eyes.'

'OK. Give me half an hour. That's how long it will take.'

'Half an *hour*?' He glared at her, then fished into his pocket and forced a tissue into her hand. 'Here, wipe your mouth with this.'

She was too angry to answer. She grabbed the tissue and wiped it across her face. Lipstick smeared onto her cheeks.

'Afra, don't *do* this,' he hissed at her.

'Don't do what?' she pretended to be puzzled.

He grabbed her arm suddenly and began to walk off, half dragging her behind him.

'OK,' he said. 'If you want to look a guy, it's fine by me.'

Joseph was waiting for them by the gate. As Afra walked out into the road beside him, she caught him casting sidelong glances at her. In the dark it was hard to read his expression. Surreptitiously, she pulled the tissue out again and wiped her mouth and cheeks more carefully. Even in this furious mood she couldn't face walking into a posh hotel with her face daubed with pink.

It was a short walk along the road to the hotel drive. They marched in silence up to the brightly lit building.

The foyer of the hotel was crowded with foreign holidaymakers, the men in loud coloured beach shirts, the women in skimpy sundresses, their exposed skin red with sunburn.

Afra was sick with dread. Nothing in her whole life up to now had prepared her for this. She had no idea what to do.

Minette was waiting for them, sitting on a blue sofa beside a fountain. She was wearing a turquoise trouser suit, and big earrings to match. She stood up when she saw them coming and walked over to greet them, her gilded slippers tapping on the polished marble floor.

Prof bent down to kiss her cheek. Afra clenched her fists so tightly that her fingernails dug into her palms, almost breaking through the skin. Minette disengaged herself and looked down at Afra. A peculiar expression crossed her face.

Afra opened her eyes wide and stared back at her.

She thinks I look terrible, she thought. She's despising me. So who cares? I despise her more.

She stole a sideways glance at a picture hanging on the wall nearby. She could just make out her reflection in the glass. Blood rushed up to her face. Beside Minette, she looked a total mess. Why hadn't she cleaned the lipstick off properly? There were still pink gashes across her face. And how could she have thought that Joseph's beads would look right with this shirt? They just seemed cheap and gaudy.

Minette was still looking at her. Afra's eyes narrowed. She wouldn't allow her one second of triumph, one moment of satisfaction. She tossed her head, pushed her long sleeves up to her elbows and said, in as cool a voice as she could manage, 'Thank you for your present. I'm sorry I can't accept it. Turtles are an endangered species and I don't agree—' Her voice trembled as she felt rage welling up inside her and tried to suppress it. 'I couldn't possibly own anything, *touch* anything, made of turtle shell.'

There was an awkward silence, then Minette's irritating tinkling laugh rang out.

'*Non, non*, it's not turtle shell,' she said. 'It's

only imitation. I wouldn't buy the real thing, either. It's an antique actually. I found it in a boutique in Paris. There was a fashion in the 1930s – it's a kind of cellulose I think. I've kept my earrings in it up to now, but I just thought it might have amused you.'

She was smiling down at Afra, her head on one side, trying to look winning.

'It didn't,' Afra snapped out sharply, then shut her mouth, afraid of losing her temper completely.

Prof glared at her, and put his arm through Minette's. He began to lead the way towards the restaurant.

'Well,' he said trying to sound breezy. 'Let's go check out this famous buffet, shall we? I'm so hungry I could eat a—' He checked himself and looked at Afra warily. 'A very big mound of fruit and vegetables.'

Now he's laughing at me, she thought murderously.

The food on the long buffet, that stretched from one end of the dining hall to the other, was the most sumptuous Afra had ever seen, but the very sight of it made her feel sick. The hotel kitchens might have cooked and prepared it, but it was Minette's food, in Minette's place, and the thought of allowing any of it to pass her lips filled her with revulsion. While Joseph and Prof piled their plates high with pieces of chicken and fish in subtle sauces, succulent crayfish, mounds of salad, heaps of tender young vegetables and baby new potatoes, Afra carefully selected two small tomatoes and put them on her plate with a plain bread roll.

'Is that all you want?' Minette said, as she returned to the table.

'Yes.' Afra raised her burning eyes to Minette's face and saw with pleasure the dismay in them.

Now she knows, she thought. She knows I hate her.

Prof kept the conversation going. For once he didn't say a word about archaeology. He twirled the stem of his wine glass in his hand, looked at Minette, and told stories about his travels, about the time he'd fallen asleep on a train in India and gone two hundred miles past his destination, of the moment when he'd nearly trodden on a cobra in a forest in Uganda, of the time he'd been flying across the Sahara desert, and one of the plane's engines had caught fire, and they'd crash-landed in the dunes.

'They didn't find us till the next day,' he said. 'Our water had already run out. I thought I was dead meat that time.'

'Tell us about your first time in Ethiopia, Prof,' Afra said sweetly. 'The time when you met my mother.'

He looked at her, his expression unreadable.

'You know that story, honey. I don't need to tell it again.'

Minette pushed her chair back with a clatter.

'If we've all had enough to eat,' she said brightly, 'let's go down to the beach. You can walk back to your guest house that way. The moon's nearly full tonight. It'll be lovely down there, by the water.'

6

THE TURTLE PATROL

It was a relief to get out of the dining room, away from the bright lights and the overwhelming buffet.

'Can you wait here a moment?' Minette said, when they reached the top of the path leading down through the hotel grounds to the sea. 'I just need to fetch Hani.'

Who's Hani? thought Afra suspiciously, half afraid that another Minette would appear, to double the threat. She was glad when Joseph asked the question out loud.

'My dog,' said Minette. 'It was too hot for him on the beach this morning, and he's not allowed in the dining room. He needs a run. I'll be quick.'

She disappeared through a door into one of the hotel's long corridors.

An uneasy silence fell. Prof seemed about to say something, then checked himself and began to hum an irritating tune. Afra thought of the hundred things she'd been burning to say, and couldn't bring out any of them. Joseph peered down the dimly lit path towards the beach, from which came the constant low murmur of the sea.

Minette appeared again, a little chestnut dachshund running at her heels. He looked sleek and healthy. His comical little tail wagged furiously as he sniffed at Afra's sandalled feet, then he looked up at her, as if asking to be stroked. She resisted him. He was Minette's, and she didn't want to like him.

Prof and Joseph had already set off down the path. Afra followed them, not wanting to be left behind with Minette.

The moon was nearly full, sailing across a near cloudless sky against a backdrop of sparkling stars. The light it cast was so strong that the beach of white sand seemed almost luminous. A warm southerly wind rattled the fronds of the coconut trees that fringed the beach, and the foaming edges of the waves formed long white strips as they rolled to and fro across the sand. As Afra's eyes adjusted to the light she could see that things were moving about at the edge of the water – scuttling, pale shapes. Hani dashed towards them and came back a moment later with something in his mouth.

Minette clicked her tongue.

'*Méchant*, Hani,' she said. 'Drop it.' She had been walking beside Prof and looked up at him apologetically. 'Ghost crabs,' she said. 'He loves them.'

They began to walk along the beach, away from the voices and music. Prof and Minette walked in front. Their gait was stiff and self-conscious, and they said very little to each other.

They know I'm watching them, thought Afra, with bitter satisfaction, wishing that the glares she was giving them would drill holes in their backs.

Hani, ecstatic at being taken for a walk, was making excited yapping noises, digging furiously for a second or two at a crab hole, then giving up and making short dashes into the water.

'Here, Hani! Come here. Good dog,' Joseph was saying, trying to make friends. He picked up a stick and threw it, and Hani raced for it with yelps of pleasure.

'You have a friend for life,' said Minette, turning to smile at Joseph. 'He won't let you stop now.'

Not looking where she was going, she stepped accidentally into a depression in the sand and stumbled. In an instant, Prof's arm had shot out to steady her, and for a moment it was round her waist and she was leaning against him.

Afra squeezed her eyes tight shut. She couldn't bear to look at them. Hatred, rage and misery boiled around inside her.

'Hey, Afra,' Joseph said in a low, scared voice. 'Someone is following us.'

Her eyes flew open and she turned round. Three dark shapes were walking quickly towards them.

They looked threatening in the dim light. She forgot everything else in a spurt of fear.

'Prof, Prof!' she hissed. 'Someone's behind us!'

Prof and Minette stopped and turned. Afra could feel Joseph balling his fists and tensing his muscles beside her. Then a cheerful female voice called, 'Joseph, Afra, is that you?' and Grace Otieno, flanked by Abel and Massoud, came up to them.

Joseph let out his breath in a gust of relief.

'You frightened me,' he admitted.

Grace patted his arm.

'Eh, it is the first time I have frightened anyone, except for poachers. No, you should not be afraid. This beach is very safe. My rangers and sometimes I myself, we patrol it nightly.'

She was looking curiously at Prof and Minette.

'This is my dad,' Afra said unwillingly.

There was an awkward pause.

'I'm Richard,' said Prof, holding out his hand, 'and this is Minette.'

'I am Grace Otieno,' said Grace, shaking Prof's hand.

Even in the moonlight, Afra could see that Prof was looking puzzled.

'Excuse me asking,' he said, 'but if the beach is safe, why are you patrolling it?'

Grace laughed.

'We are not looking for criminals, if that is

what you are thinking. We are looking out for turtles.'

'Turtles?' Afra said eagerly.

'Yes. It is at night-time that the females come up the beach to lay their eggs. But they can easily be disturbed. If people are around, and if they make a noise or come too closely to look at them—' she broke off, as Hani dashed back from an exploration he had been making in the sand dunes, and bounced around near her feet, yapping shrilly, 'or if dogs interfere with them, they will just return back to the sea, and they may drop their eggs into the water, and the whole clutch will be lost.'

'That's awful,' breathed Afra. 'So people should keep off the beach at night? We shouldn't be here either?'

'If you are quiet, and look out for turtles and their tracks, and move right out of the way when you see one, and don't take flash pictures or use torches, it is OK,' Grace said. She looked apologetically at Minette. 'But it is better not to bring a dog.'

'Oh! I'm sorry. I didn't know,' said Minette hastily. 'Hani, come here! Come here, Hani!'

She pulled a lead out of her pocket and clipped it into Hani's collar. The little dog whined and pulled away from her.

'I'll take him back to the hotel,' Minette said.

Afra felt a quickening of hope.

'I'll come with you,' said Prof. 'That path's too dark for you to manage on your own. Wait here, you two. I won't be long.'

A knife turned in Afra's stomach.

'Can we come with you, on your patrol?' Joseph was asking Grace.

Grace looked doubtful.

'We will go a long way,' she said, 'and we will not come back in this direction. You would have to return alone. It is better for you to wait here.'

Massoud and Abel were already walking on down the beach. Grace hurried to catch them up, and a moment later the three of them were no more than dark shadows moving away across the sand.

A rumbling belch broke from Joseph.

'That was a good dinner,' he said. 'One of the best I've ever had. Why didn't you eat anything?'

'I couldn't.' Afra shuddered. 'I would have thrown up.'

'Minette's not that bad,' Joseph said. 'She could have been worse. And you were really rude to her.'

'Joseph,' said Afra, 'if you say another word about that – that woman, I'll kill you. I really will.'

Silence descended. The only sound was the soft shirring of the waves and the clattering rustle of the wind in the palms. Then suddenly, loud thumping music burst out into the night. An echoing beat sent some roosting birds fluttering restlessly in the trees, and a high wailing voice rang out across the water. It was coming from behind them, from the strip of beach that fronted the hotel grounds.

'It's enough to scare any turtle for miles around,' said Joseph.

Afra drew in her breath.

'You're right. It's awful.'

She saw the turtle in her mind's eye again, spiralling gracefully upwards through the water. Perhaps she was there now, out on the reef, her eggs heavy inside her, waiting to make the dangerous ascent of the beach. She would be accustomed to many sounds, to the pounding of surf on rocky shores, to the pattering of rain on the sea's surface, to the howling of the wind in violent storms, even to the whistling and clicking of whales calling to each other in the deep ocean, but this alien sound, this amplified human music, would surely confuse and frighten her. She might turn back, and lose her precious burden in the water.

Afra gritted her teeth and set off at a trot along the beach.

'Come on, Joseph,' she said over her shoulder. 'We've got to stop them!'

Joseph ran to catch her up.

'Afra, are you crazy? They won't listen to us.

They might turn nasty or something. Stop, Afra, listen!'

But Afra was flying along the beach as if on winged feet, the heavy beads flopping against her chest. She could see people ahead of her now. They were dancing about on the sand, bottles in their hands, shouting and laughing above the beat of the music, illuminated by the necklace of lights strung along the shoreline at the edge of the hotel grounds.

All the misery of the day seemed to fuse within Afra, and turned into a burning anger. Without pausing for a moment to think out a plan of campaign, she rushed into the middle of the dancers shouting, 'Stop! Stop it! Turn the music off!'

People turned to look at her. Most stopped dancing. Someone found the switch on the sound system and snapped it off. They crowded round Afra.

'What's the matter?' someone said. 'Is something wrong? Is someone hurt?'

'The noise?' said Afra, frowning fiercely. 'Don't you realize? Turtles are coming up to lay their eggs on this beach. You'll scare them away!'

Several people burst out laughing.

'Turtles! Did you hear that, you guys? We'll scare the turtles!'

'Yeah,' one boy said to another. 'With your ugly mug you'd scare anything.'

'I'll scare you, mate, anyway,' the second boy said, trying to get the first one's head in an armlock.

'Listen! *Listen*!' Afra shouted, shaking off Joseph who, stiff with embarrassment, was trying to pull her away. 'The turtles get scared if they hear noises. They might just go back out to sea!'

One girl said, 'Are there really turtles along here? I wouldn't mind going to have a look. Want to come anyone? Let's all go on a turtle hunt! They're huge. I've seen pictures of them. You can ride on their backs. Where's my camera?'

'No!' Afra practically screamed. 'Don't you understand? You have to give them space! Leave them alone!'

'I've had enough of this,' someone said angrily. 'Why don't you leave us alone? Push off, you two. Turn the music up again, Charlie.'

The music blared out again, louder than ever.

Afra felt Joseph's hand on her arm again.

'This is useless,' he said. 'Come on.'

Afra felt tears welling up in her eyes. She dashed them away.

'They're *monsters*,' she said. '*Vandals*.'

She let Joseph lead her away, back along the beach. Thick piles of seaweed had been washed up here, and her feet slipped on a wet patch. She fell to her knees. For a moment, she wanted just to give up, to lie down on the ground and scream and cry, like a toddler having a tantrum, but then she realized that something had changed. The music was quieter. It was going slower and slower, grinding down to a halt.

Their batteries have run out, she told herself triumphantly. Serve them right.

Joseph was striding on, his shape almost disappearing in the shadowy light. She ran after him.

'Did you hear that?' she said. 'Their batteries just went flat.'

He didn't answer.

'Joseph?' she sounded anxious. 'What's bothering you? Are you mad with me?'

He turned and looked at her.

'Am I mad with you? What do you think, Afra? You've been awful, just horrible, all day. And the way you talked to those people – it was just so stupid! So crazy! Did you really think they would listen to you, screaming and shouting like that? I felt – I felt ashamed!'

'Oh boy.' She was shaking her head, like a dog trying to shake off a shower of cold water. 'Oh wow. I guess I deserved that. It was – I just – it's been a horrible day, Joseph. It was almost the worst ever, in my whole life. I'm sorry. I was dumb, back there. I should have stopped to think.'

Her contrition seemed to touch him. He put his hands on her shoulders and gave her a friendly shake.

'You never do stop to think, Afra. I'd get

worried if you ever did. It would be like a personality change or something.'

She laughed shakily, trying to think of something funny and nice to say, but before she had a chance, she became aware of three figures, coming up fast towards them across the moonlit beach. Grace and the rangers had turned back.

'Joseph! Afra!' panted Grace. 'We came to find you. There's a turtle down there, about two hundred metres from here, back that way, towards the guest house. It came out of the water and heard the noise and went back into the sea again. I want you to watch out for her for me. If you see her, keep well away. Don't go anywhere near, or make a noise. Just make sure nobody else comes up to disturb her. I'm going to talk to those people who have been making all that noise. I'm going to ask them for their cooperation.'

7

AN ARDUOUS CLIMB

Afra felt chastened as she trotted back along the beach behind Joseph.

I've messed up everything today, she thought.

The idea depressed her. Usually, when she was feeling bad, she'd let anger take the place of unhappiness, and it would grow and grow and shoot out in a volcanic eruption. It would quickly burn itself out and she'd feel better. But she'd exploded already, in front of all those tourists. It had only irritated them and done more harm than good. And she'd ended up by feeling worse.

Joseph halted suddenly and she nearly bumped into him.

'What are we looking for?' he said. 'I mean, we don't even know where the turtle came out of the water in the first place.'

Afra considered this, glad to think about something new.

'They leave tracks, though, don't they?' she said. 'We'll see them in the sand.'

'Oh yes. Of course. I didn't think of that.'

He set off again.

At least I got something right, thought Afra.

It was a small triumph, but better than nothing. She began to feel a little better.

The tracks, when they found them, were so big that they were easy to see even in the moonlight, but they almost walked right across them, mistaking them for tyre marks. They realized at the same moment, and stopped dead, looking up the beach to where the turtle's trail abruptly stopped, and down again towards the sea, where the return tracks ended at the water's edge.

'This is Mr Mohammed's bit of beach,' exclaimed Afra. 'We're almost home.' She pointed to a gap in the dunes where a few low lights shone down onto the beach. 'Look, that's where the steps go up. It's so different at night, it's kind of hard to tell.'

Joseph was studying the turtle's tracks.

'I thought they were from a car or something,' he said, 'but they're not really like that at all. They're beautiful.'

It was easy to read the turtle's movements from the tracks. The smooth centre showed where the heavy undershell had been dragged across the beach, and on either side regular ruts revealed where the flippers had flailed against the sand.

Afra and Joseph had bent down to study the tracks but now they both stood up and looked expectantly towards the sea.

'Do you think she'll come out at the same place

again?' said Afra, her voice unconsciously dropping to a whisper.

'I don't know. Maybe. We'd better wait here, anyway. What about Prof and Minette? Perhaps they won't find us. They'll be worried.'

Afra wanted to say, I don't care if they don't find us at all. I don't care if they get really upset and think I ran away, but she didn't want to annoy Joseph again.

'We're not far from the hotel here,' she said. 'They'll just think we've gone home. Or they'll see Grace and she'll tell them.'

They sat down on the sand and trained their eyes on the edge of the sea. At any moment, something might emerge from its depths, one of the earth's great travellers, mysterious, beautiful, more ancient than the dinosaurs.

The frothing white edges of the rolling waves advanced and retreated, advanced and retreated with mesmerizing regularity. Afra emptied her mind as she watched them. It seemed after a few minutes that she'd been here for a very long time, and that she would stay here for ages to come, for ever, perhaps . . .

In her dreamy state she saw something black and rounded form itself out of the water. It had appeared from nowhere, rising up as if it had been created at that very moment. She saw a head rear up, ending in beaked mouth, almost like a hawk's.

'It's a turtle!' she gasped, grabbing Joseph's arm. 'Look, there! She's coming!'

Without another word they both began to slide, with infinite caution, backwards along the sand, away from the turtle's route to the top of the beach. Then, well away, but still close enough to see, they settled down to watch, keeping absolutely silent and still.

The turtle paused for a moment at the water's edge, then, as if reassured that she was alone and would be undisturbed, she began her laborious ascent of the beach. Her flippers, which moved so gracefully and with such subtlety and strength in the water, seemed feeble on land. They beat against the resisting sand, every thrust consuming the creature's energy and strength, while propelling her only a few centimetres towards her goal.

'She's not going to make it,' breathed Afra. 'It's too far.'

Joseph didn't answer and she sensed that he, too, was willing the turtle on, living with her every step of her exhausting journey.

Afra longed to rush out and help, to wave a wand and transport the turtle somehow to a perfect nesting place, or at the very least to smooth the sand in front of her, but she sat motionless. This creature was giving birth. This was her arduous labour. She would accept no interference. She had to do it alone.

Slowly, agonizingly, the turtle was inching up

the beach. The moonlight glistened on her lovely wet carapace, the jagged edges of which made shallow subsidiary trails through the sand. Several times she rested, lying awkwardly straddled, her head drooping, her flippers still, and each time Afra held her breath, afraid that she would never move again. But each time the turtle seemed to summon up fresh reserves of strength and struggled on.

She had nearly reached the top of the beach, where the low sand dunes, under a light covering of coarse grasses and fleshy leafed creepers, covered the site she had chosen. With one last immense effort, she heaved her great body up onto it, and began to dig.

'Afra! Joseph!'

Prof's voice cut through the night air like the blast of a trumpet. Afra shot to her feet and rushed towards the sound.

'Sh! Quiet!' she hissed in a violent whisper.

She could see them now, Prof and Minette, walking unconcernedly towards her across the beach. She dashed up to them.

'A turtle's come up to lay,' she whispered. 'We mustn't make a single sound or she'll hear us and give up and go back to the sea.'

'Where? Where is she?' Prof whispered back.

'Up there. On the dune. We watched her crawl all the way up the beach.'

She crept back on silent feet to where Joseph

was still sitting. Prof and Minette followed soundlessly, and the four of them sat still, waiting, peering up towards the moonlit dunes.

For a few long minutes, Afra thought she must have dreamed the whole thing. There was no sign of movement from the dunes, and the round dark shape of the turtle was hard to pick out from this distance among the many shadows and dips in the sand.

Then the turtle began to dig. The watchers on the beach couldn't see her now, but they could see silvery showers of sand as her flippers scooped at it and sent it flying. They could hear her making groaning noises, too, as the breath was forced out of her by her gigantic efforts. Once, Prof cleared his throat a little too loudly, and once Minette shifted her hand suddenly so that her bangles jingled. Afra wanted to snap out at them, but she restrained herself. Anyway, the turtle was making so much noise, as she sent the sand flying in all directions, that it was unlikely such small sounds could disturb her.

The murmur of low voices came from behind, and Afra turned to see Grace and the two rangers approaching. She signalled to them and they saw her and came up quietly.

'She's there,' whispered Afra. 'In the dunes.'

She heard Grace grunt with annoyance.

'Too near the path where Mr Mohammed keeps his boat. And the lights on the steps will confuse the hatchlings. It's a bad place,' she said, as if to herself.

'You mean it's all wasted? All her effort?' Afra sensed that her voice was rising with distress and made an effort to keep it low.

'No.' Grace shook her head. 'It will not be wasted, but we might have to translocate it to give the hatchlings a chance. We'll check it once she is laying.'

'You won't wait till she's finished?' murmured Prof. 'Won't we put her off if we go too close now?'

'No.' Grace shook her head. 'Once a turtle has made her nest and begun to lay, she seems to go into a trance. She is not aware of anything around her. But we'll approach her carefully. We won't go close.'

For a few moments now the showers of sand had stopped.

'Is she laying yet?' Afra asked. She was half eager to go nearer, and half reluctant. She was afraid, in spite of what Grace had said, that the turtle would be distressed by the presence of human beings.

'She won't be laying yet,' Grace said. 'She has finished making her body pit, but now she is scooping out the deep hole for her eggs. It will be perfectly round. Beautifully shaped.'

Minutes passed. No one spoke. At last, Grace gave a quiet command to Abel, and he disappeared on bare noiseless feet towards the labouring turtle. He was back a moment later.

'She is laying,' he said.

Grace stood up.

'Stay behind me,' she said. 'Don't speak or make a noise.'

Everyone stood up, and in single file followed Grace. She halted near the dunes and crouched down. Afra had been behind her, but she could see the turtle clearly now, about five metres away. She had hollowed out a great dip in the sand, and at one side of it she had made a deep, perfectly round hole.

She lay still, her flippers braced against the sand. Her tail was suspended over the hole and beneath it she was dropping, one after the other, perfect, white, round eggs, the size of large plums. She seemed unaware of the watchers. She was absorbed, working, her painful journey up the beach completed, her nest made.

Then Afra saw that tears were spilling out of the turtle's eyes and were running down her face.

She can't be crying, not really, she said to herself, but she felt a kind of awe, the memory of an old pain.

My mother laboured for me, she thought, and then she died.

The eggs were still falling, soundlessly, into the nest the turtle had made for them. Afra watched each one with an upsurge of wordless love. This mother was suffering for them now, but she would not be here when they emerged, as they soon would, defenceless and inexperienced, into the world, to make their own perilous way down the beach and into the wide ocean.

I wish I could help you, she thought. I do so want to help you.

The last egg fell, pale and gleaming, and at once the turtle began her work again. With wide sweeps of her flippers she was filling in the nest hole, then piling the sand over the hollow, working skilfully, instinctively, to hide her brood from the many predators who would try to destroy it.

She finished at last. Slowly, with terrible weariness, she began her descent to the sea, and the watchers sat in respectful silence, no one saying a word, until at last she reached the water's edge and, with a sudden spurt of energy and an instant return of her natural grace and lightness, she disappeared into the warm welcoming water.

8

THE PARTY-GOERS

For a long moment, no one moved. Then Afra said, 'Did you see? She was crying.'

'Not crying,' said Grace. 'Not like us. It is just that water comes out of their eyes to wash out the salt. But if it was me, and I had done all that, I would be crying!'

She stood up, and straightened a crick in her back.

'Eh, I am too old for all this running around in the night. And this turtle mother, she has not been intelligent. She has planted her nest too close to the path. Abel, what do you think? Will we have to move it?'

Abel, the taller of the two rangers, walked around the nest, assessing it.

'It is always a little risky, to move the eggs,' he said.

'Why?' asked Afra eagerly. 'We'd help. We'd be very careful. We could—'

Grace shook her head.

'It's not so easy. The turtle mother is very clever. She made her hole at the exact right depth to keep the eggs at a precise temperature. She even dropped them in such a way that the air can circulate round them and keep them fresh. The yolk sacs are so delicate. It is easy to kill the eggs if they are turned over.'

'I didn't know all that.' Afra bit her lip.

'Well,' said Grace, relenting, 'it's not easy to know all those things, but it's not easy to move a nest, either.'

'Perhaps we should move the path,' said Prof jokingly.

'Yes!' Afra leaped in again. 'We could *easily* do that. We could smooth out a new way for the boat, just till the eggs hatch, and then we could build up a barricade round the nest or something. You know, to warn people off.'

Even in the moonlight, she could see that a relieved smile had spread over Grace's tired face.

'Now that is a good idea,' she said. 'And you will save us a lot of difficult work, and an even later night. The eggs have to be moved in the first few hours after they are laid. We would have had to do the whole job now. We couldn't even have waited till morning.'

Abel looked dissatisfied.

'The lights,' he murmured in Swahili. 'There are still the lights.'

Joseph looked up at the light streaming out from Mr Mohammed's guest house, and at the lamps illuminating the path to the beach.

'But they don't matter now, do they?' he said,

had dropped Afra's arm but now she caught hold of his and held on to it tightly.

The tourists had left the beach. The lights strung along the shore lit the churned-up sand and gleamed on glass where empty bottles had been thrown down.

Afra was about to say, hey, they're not here any more, so I guess we'd better go home, when Minette took the words out of her mouth.

'They've gone,' she said, with her grating little laugh. '*C'est bien*. You can go home.'

Afra's hackles rose immediately.

'Wait,' she said. 'I can hear them. They just moved back off the beach a little way. They're up there now, under the trees.'

She took a deep breath, screwed up her courage and marched off in the direction of the music.

'Richard,' she heard Minette say behind her. 'Are you going to let her do this? They've been drinking. They could turn nasty.'

'You don't know Afra,' said Prof, and Afra felt a thrill of pleasure at the pride in his voice. 'Once she decides to do something, it takes an earth-quake to stop her.'

Some of the tourists were still dancing, gyrating to the heavy beat that was pouring out of the portable stereo. Several others had given up and were sitting around under the trees, talking and laughing. A camper's lamp hung from a low branch, bathing them in light and casting deep shadows beyond them.

They looked up as Afra stepped into the circle of light.

'Well, look who's here!' one of the boys said, standing up and coming towards Afra. 'Little Miss Know-it-all.'

She steeled herself not to back away.

'Hi,' she said, a little breathlessly. 'I came, I just came to say sorry. I guess I was – you know – kind of aggressive back then.'

One of the girls called out, 'What does the kid want, Barney? Have we been upsetting the poor little birds and bees again?'

Afra made herself walk towards the girl.

'Hi,' she said again. 'I just came to say I was over the top, about the turtles, I mean. What I mean to say is, I got kind of upset, just worried about them, you know.'

The girl shrugged.

'That's OK. Some woman came along with a couple of guys, and explained about them laying eggs and stuff. They sound cute.' She leaned forward and stared at Afra more closely. 'Hey, what have you done to your eyes?'

Afra's hand shot up to her face and brushed against her eyelashes, which were thick with mascara.

The girl sat back again.

'It's just your make-up. It's run a bit. It does

that to me all the time here. It's the heat. You get all sweaty and the next minute you've got stuff running down your cheeks.'

Afra felt herself blushing and started wiping her cheeks with her fingers. The girl laughed.

'Don't worry. It hasn't run that much. You look kind of sweet. Like a panda.'

Afra didn't know what to say. Things weren't turning out at all the way she had expected. Another boy and girl strolled up to her, and she could see Prof and Minette on the edge of the circle talking and laughing with some of the others.

'What happened then?' the boy said. 'Did you see your turtle, or what?'

'Yeah.' Afra was beginning to relax, and her smile was genuine this time. 'It was so incredible. She—'

'How did you know it was a female?' the girl interrupted.

The boy laughed.

'Because she'd come up to lay eggs, fluffhead,' he said, draping his arm fondly round the girl's shoulders.

'Yes, that's right. She did,' said Afra. 'Laid her eggs, I mean. It was so great. She came out of the sea, and looked round for a second, just checking it was all OK, and then she struggled all the way up the beach.'

'Did you go up to her?' another boy said. 'I heard you could ride them.'

Afra swallowed hard and kept the smile pinned to her face.

'No. They get distressed easily. If they're disturbed they just go back to the sea and let the eggs out into the water, and they all die. You have to keep right away from them and not make a sound.'

'That's what the lady said, Steve,' the first girl said. 'You should try taking the cotton wool out of your ears.'

'Do it for me, darlin',' said Steve, putting his head down in the girl's lap and grinning up at her.

She squealed and pushed him away.

'Anyway,' said Afra awkwardly, 'she got up the beach OK, and made her nest and everything. I just came back to say thank you, you know, for giving her space.'

'Nah, no problem,' said the boy called Barney. 'Glad we could help. Have a beer.'

'Barney!' the first girl said. 'She's a kid! How old are you?'

'Twelve,' said Afra unwillingly.

'Twelve!' the girl looked at her admiringly. 'You've got bottle, for a twelve-year-old.'

'Thanks,' said Afra.

Prof strolled up.

'Are you ready, honey? Shall we go?'

'Yeah.' Afra was suddenly feeling exhausted.

'Are you off then?' said the girl. 'Wow. Wish I'd seen your turtle. They don't come up in the daytime, do they?'

'No,' said Afra. 'Only at night.'

'Just as well. We couldn't creep around the beach all day, trying not to upset the turtles. Barney here would go off his trolley. If he's not making a noise, he thinks he's died. Goodnight, kid. See you around.'

9

AFRA IS PERSUASIVE

After the many humiliations of the day, Afra slept badly. Uncomfortable dreams and sad thoughts chased each other through her head all night and she woke early, glad that the day had come.

She lay in bed for a while. A branch of brilliant purple bougainvillea flowers half covered her window and she watched it unseeingly for a while.

Why did *she* have to come and spoil everything? she thought. We were just fine the way we were.

Pink clouds dotted the sky beyond the purple flowers. Afra lifted her arm to look at her watch. Six-thirty. The sun must have risen only a few minutes ago. The beach would be deserted. Perhaps, after all the humans had gone to bed last night, other turtles had come up to make their nests. Their tracks might still be visible.

She jumped out of bed, threw on her clothes and let herself out of her room, trying not to wake Prof and Joseph in their little cabins nearby. She wanted to be alone.

Mr Mohammed was squatting beside his

generator, fiddling with the guts of the machine. Afra hesitated.

I ought to ask him about making a new path, she thought, but she wanted badly to go down to the beach, and she trotted past him and ran on down the steps.

The tide was far out now. The wind had dropped and the air still held the delicious coolness of dawn. Round fluffy clouds of every colour, from the palest pink to a deep golden orange, drifted across a sky which was the softest imaginable blue. The sea rocked lazily backwards and forwards onto the white sand, leaving patches of dark seaweed as it retreated. Further out, the water was a perfect aquamarine, merging in places to a deep royal blue. A few waders darted about at the water's edge, while clouds of ghost crabs, pale as paper, scuttled across the freshly washed sand.

Afra drew a deep breath. Yesterday had been horrible, practically the worst day of her life. Perhaps things would be better today. Perhaps Minette would disappear back to wherever she had come from. Maybe Prof himself would take her and Joseph snorkelling. If she was lucky, she might even see another turtle. Anyway, on this perfect morning, on this wide empty beach, beside the sparkling ocean, it was impossible not to feel a little bit happy.

The tracks that last night's turtle had made had

been all but obliterated by the tide and the wind. She could see the nest clearly though. It was a dip in the low dune, free of the scanty vegetation that covered the sand on either side. She went up to inspect it more closely. It looked dull and ordinary in the bright light of day. It was hard to believe that down there, just under the surface, dozens of perfect white eggs lay, and that inside them an amazing transformation was taking place, as miniature turtles formed themselves from the tiny seeds within.

She could see now that Grace had been right. The nest was awkwardly placed. Mr Mohammed's grey inflatable, which he kept for the use of his guests, was pulled up just beyond it. Someone carrying it down would run along the path he had carefully made, right beside the nest. One careless step would push down the sand and crush the delicate eggs. It gave Afra the shivers to think of it.

She left the nest and set off along the beach towards the KWS compound. It wasn't far. She looked carefully as she went, but saw no other signs of turtle tracks or nests.

Hunger suddenly assailed her. She had had almost no supper last night, and no breakfast this morning. She turned and began to trot back towards the guest house.

She arrived out of breath to find Joseph already outside the dining room, talking to Mr

Mohammed. Joseph was tense and frowning, his chin jutting forward as if he had been arguing. Mr Mohammed had his hands on his hips, his plump tummy was jutting out under his long shirt, and his round face was filled with irritation.

'A turtle nest? Right where I keep my boat? It must be moved! I can't have it there,' he was saying.

Joseph heard Afra coming, and turned to give her a warning look.

He thinks I'm going to lose my temper, she thought. I'll show him.

'Hi, Mr Mohammed,' she said brightly. 'Is there some of your yummy papaya for breakfast? I'm just starving.'

Mr Mohammed smiled at her. He was proud of his food and liked it to be appreciated.

'I picked a papaya from my own tree this very morning,' he said. 'It's a perfect one. Everything's ready, in there.' He jerked a thumb towards the dining room. 'There's toast, tea, coffee, eggs – whatever you like.'

'Wow. Brilliant,' said Afra enthusiastically. She felt Joseph's astonished eyes on her and ignored him. 'I just went down to the beach, Mr Mohammed. It's so lovely here. You have the nicest place on the whole coast, I bet.'

Mr Mohammed beamed with pleasure.

'It was my father's,' he said, 'and his father's before that. They were fishermen, but I could see, when the trawlers began to come, that it would be hard times for us. Visitors! I said to myself. Tourists! That's the future. I built this place alone, I myself, every bit of it.'

'It's so great,' said Afra, smiling sunnily at him. 'And the best thing is, there's so much wildlife here. You know what, when Joseph's uncle took us snorkelling yesterday, I saw a stingray.'

'A stingray?' Mr Mohammed laughed indulgently. 'When I was a boy, there was so much more here. The fish, they were like grains of sand. You couldn't count them. Octopuses the size of children, big cowries and spider shells everywhere you looked, turtles—'

'Turtles!' cried Afra. 'That's so brilliant. We saw one last night, Mr Mohammed. She made a nest right here beside your slipway. I didn't know you had *turtles* coming on to your beach. I'm going to tell all my friends, and their parents, when I go home to Nairobi. They won't believe it. They'd all come here if they knew there were turtles, nesting right down below your guest house.'

Mr Mohammed shook his head doubtfully.

'There are turtles everywhere along the coast,' he said. 'They're nothing special.'

'There *were* turtles everywhere,' Afra gently corrected him. 'But Mrs Otieno – do you know her? – she said they've become very rare, because the trawlers catch them, and their nests are always being disturbed so the babies don't hatch. I guess the turtle we saw last night was real clever, making her nest right beside your house, where she'll be quite, quite safe!'

For a moment, she was afraid she'd gone too far. Mr Mohammed's brown eyes looked down shrewdly into hers and he pursed his plummy lips. Then he passed a hand over the shiny brown skin on his bald crown and burst out laughing.

'You kids! You and your turtles! You are too much for one old man. Go and eat your breakfast.'

Afra hesitated. She wanted to push him, to ask him straight out to let them make a new path and block up the old one, but instinct told her to hold back. She skipped on into the dining room in a way which, she fondly hoped, would look charming and little-girly.

Joseph followed her and they sat down together at the table. He was holding himself in, desperately trying not to laugh.

'Afra,' he wheezed at last. 'You are so awful! I can't believe that was really you.'

She beamed at him.

'It sort of worked though, don't you think? I mean, at least he's thinking about it. You were just getting him all bothered. You know, Joseph, it's no good losing your temper with people. It just doesn't help at all.'

The affected saintliness in her voice goaded him

into making the worst face he could imagine, crossing his eyes and sticking out his tongue. She burst out laughing.

'I'm glad you're feeling so cheerful this morning,' Prof's voice broke in.

Afra looked up at him quickly, then dropped her eyes to the juicy slice of papaya on her plate. She wasn't sure how to face him today.

'You look happier than poor Mr Mohammed, anyway,' Prof went on. 'He's been telling me he'll need to make a new path for his boat, just when he'd finished work on the old one.'

Afra and Joseph exchanged triumphant looks.

'We'll help,' Joseph said.

'I've been down to look at it already,' said Afra.

'I'm not doing anything till I've had my breakfast,' Prof said firmly, sitting down and reaching for the coffee pot.

'You mean you'll come too?' exclaimed Afra, delighted. 'That's great, Prof. We'll do it together.'

It was easier than Afra had thought to clear away the vegetation further along the dune and level off a new place where Mr Mohammed's boat could easily be carried down to the beach. They all worked hard for a couple of hours, while Mr Mohammed himself bobbed around anxiously, directing operations.

They'd nearly finished when Afra stood up, wiping the sweat off her face with her sleeve. She stepped back to admire their work, and jumped with alarm as something touched her ankle. She looked down. Hani was sniffing around her feet, his silky ears flopping over his nose.

She looked up and scowled as she saw Minette coming down the beach towards them. Minette was wearing yet another outfit this morning, a pair of blue trousers with a big, perfectly ironed white shirt. A broad brimmed straw hat rested on her blonde head.

'*Bonjour*! Good morning everyone!' she called out gaily.

'Bad morning, you mean,' muttered Afra.

Minette flashed them all a wide smile, her eyes resting on Afra for a fraction longer than on the others.

'I hope you don't mind,' she said, a little anxiously. 'There was a boatman up at the hotel at breakfast this morning, offering trips out to the marine park in a glass-bottomed boat. He's the best guide, the manager said. He doesn't come to the hotel very often, so I just took a chance and booked a trip for us four this morning.'

'That's fantastic, Minette,' said Prof, a little too eagerly. 'What a great idea.'

'Thank you,' Joseph said politely.

Afra tightened her lips. There was nothing, nothing on earth she would hate more than to be stuck in a boat with Minette, a boat that had been organized by Minette, paid for by Minette, with Prof and Joseph oozing sickening gratitude all over Minette for her cleverness and enterprise.

'I'm tired,' she said shortly. 'You go. I'll stay here.'

Prof looked at her quizzically.

'You get an amazing view from a glass-bottomed boat,' he said. 'You can see everything. We might not get another chance.'

Afra glared at him.

'Don't try to bribe me,' she muttered. 'I'm not a baby.'

'What?' Prof leaned forward, trying to hear her.

'I said I'll see you later,' said Afra. 'I'm going to my room,' and she ran off up the steps to the guest house.

10

TURTLE ALERT

Afra stayed in her room until she was sure that Prof and Joseph had fetched all their things and left the guest house. She felt bitterly resentful. A trip in a glass-bottomed boat out to the marine park was a treat Prof had promised her when they'd first arrived on this holiday, and she'd been looking forward to it from the start. Now it had been unfairly snatched away, thanks to Minette, and she had the whole long morning ahead of her with nothing to do.

None of them care about me at all, she thought miserably. Prof didn't even try to persuade me. He's only interested in *her* now. He probably wouldn't notice if I ran away and disappeared for ever and ever.

She lay on her bed, curled up in a ball, and let herself cry for a while. Then she sat up and gave herself a shake.

That's what they'll expect me to do, just lie around and go all sulky, she thought.

She didn't want to give them the satisfaction. She found a tissue, wiped her eyes, blew her nose and opened the door of her room.

No one was around. Clattering sounds came from the kitchen, where someone must be preparing lunch, and voices came from the dining room.

I might as well go down to the beach, thought Afra, just for something to do.

She walked past the dining room. Grace Otieno and Mr Mohammed were sitting at the table, sipping sodas.

'Afra!' Grace called out, her full mouth curved in a tremendous smile. 'I have seen the new path you made this morning. You did a wonderful job! Come and join us!'

Afra's heart lifted. Someone wanted her company, after all. She went in and slid onto the bench beside Grace.

'This girl,' said Grace, putting an arm round Afra's shoulders, 'she loves wild things. She is a conservation expert already.'

'I know,' said Mr Mohammed, eyeing Afra cautiously. 'She persuaded me to move my path.'

Grace burst out laughing.

'You would have done it for me, Mr Mohammed, anyway,' she said. 'That's why I came along this morning, to ask you for your help in protecting the nest. Then I found the job already done.' She sipped the last of her soda and put her glass down. 'Eh, that was good, but now I must go back to my office. So much work to do!'

'Mrs Otieno,' said Afra, 'on that chart in your office there's a turtle nest that's due to hatch soon. Where is it exactly?'

Grace stood up.

'It's between the KWS compound and the village. Come with me and I'll show you.' She suddenly thought of something and sat down again. 'That reminds me, Mr Mohammed, I want to talk to you about your lights.'

'My lights?' Mr Mohammed was looking wary again. 'What's the matter with them? They are new. I installed them myself last month only.'

'It's a little difficulty only,' Grace said smoothly. 'We can think of a solution, I'm sure. The problem will come when the turtle eggs hatch. The hatchlings will be attracted to your lights instead of to the sea.'

Mr Mohammed was frowning.

'They'll soon realize their mistake,' he said. 'They'll turn round and get to the sea eventually. They always do.'

'They used to,' Grace said, 'before there were lights on the beach. It's much harder for them now.'

There was a short pause.

'The work! The money! All I have done to improve this place!' exclaimed Mr Mohammed. 'First you say, "Oh, Mr Mohammed, build your nice guest house because we need tourists to come and visit our national park and make it pay for itself," and then, when I make it beautiful for tourists, I am doing the wrong thing!'

Grace smiled soothingly, but Afra could see that under the table one hand was tightly clenched.

He's really winding her up, she thought. She wants to shout and argue, just like I do.

'The wrong thing?' Grace said peaceably. 'No! Your place here is just fine. Everything is first class. Your food! People talk about it all along the coast!'

Mr Mohammed's head tilted to one side.

'It is true that our fish sauces are the best anywhere,' he said, mollified.

'But . . .' Grace began, and paused.

Afra had a sudden idea.

'Mr Mohammed,' she said, blinding him with her smile, 'The lights would be OK, wouldn't they, if they just didn't shine down onto the beach?'

Mr Mohammed snorted.

'If they didn't shine? What is the point of having lights if they don't shine?'

'No, but they don't need to be seen all the way round. Couldn't we put a kind of shade or something on the side facing the sea? Then the lights would just fall on the steps and in the compound here, but you wouldn't see anything from the beach.'

Mr Mohammed pulled down the corners of his mouth.

'It wouldn't work. If you put shades on those lights the wind would blow them off.'

'No, but you could make little walls, like barricades,' said Afra, warming to her idea. 'Drive some sticks deep into the sand and put matting between them, or something like that.'

Mr Mohammed was still shaking his head. Afra felt exasperated. She nearly burst out, 'Don't you *want* to save the hatchlings? Don't you even want to *try*?' but she looked up and saw that Grace was giving her a tiny shake of her head.

'Maybe mine wasn't such a good idea,' said Afra meekly, 'but you're so clever, Mr Mohammed, you'll be able to think of something much better.'

She knew at once that she'd overdone it. He wagged an irritated finger at her.

'No, young lady. You think you can flatter me into doing anything you want, but I'll do what I like in my own house.'

Grace stood up again.

'Of course you will,' she said, with a conciliatory laugh. 'Thank you for the soda, Mr Mohammed. It was very welcome. Afra, do you want to come with me, to see the nest?'

Afra followed her down the steps.

'I'm sorry,' she said, as they reached the beach. 'I should have kept my big mouth shut. He'd have done it for you.'

'No, no.' Grace Otieno shook her head. 'You

don't know Mr Mohammed. He is always like that. He grumbles and fusses, and then in the end he does the right thing. Your idea was a good one. Those lights will be shaded before tonight, I am sure of it.'

'How long does it take for the eggs to hatch?' asked Afra.

'Fifty to sixty days. It depends on the temperature. They are strange creatures, turtles. The temperature of the nest is very important for them. If it is a little warmer, most of the hatchlings are males. If it is cooler, most are females.'

Afra stared at her.

'That's weird.'

'Mysterious,' nodded Grace. 'Very ancient, they are, and very mysterious.' She halted. 'Look, there's the other nest, just above the beach. We put some thorny branches round it to protect it. They are too high off the ground to bother the hatchlings, though, when they decide to emerge and make a run for the sea. They could go tonight, or tomorrow, maybe.'

'I'd so love to see them do it,' said Afra.

Grace shook her head.

'Very few people see them. They go at night, when the tide is high, and they run down the beach all together. In fifteen or twenty minutes they have reached the sea and swum away.'

She looked at her watch.

'Now I must return to my office. Are you going

back to the guest house now? Where is your friend today?'

'He went out with – with my dad,' said Afra awkwardly.

'And you didn't go?'

'No.'

Grace looked at her thoughtfully.

She's going to ask me more questions, thought Afra uncomfortably, and dropped her eyes.

Instead, Grace said, 'If you are not busy this morning, perhaps you would like to do a job for me. I want to put a poster in the hotel, to tell the tourists about the turtles, help them understand how they can help them, or at least, not disturb them. Can you draw? Could you design one for me? I'll give you some paper, if you like.'

Afra felt a glow of pleasure. She liked drawing, and knew she was good at it.

'I'd love to do that,' she said.

Half an hour later, Afra was back at the guest house, sitting at the big table in the dining room. Grace Otieno had given her a poster-sized sheet of paper, and several smaller sheets on which she could work out her design.

She sat thinking for a while, feeling a little overwhelmed by the task, when the perfect poster design leaped into her mind. She tried it out first on one of the smaller pieces of paper.

TURTLE ALERT!!! she wrote in big letters at the top.

She left a space for a picture of a turtle, and under it she wrote, 'Turtles nest above the beach in this area. They are beautiful and rare and precious, and they need peace and quiet and darkness. If you see one, please don't go near it. Just watch it quietly. Don't shine any bright lights, or make loud noises. Please try and protect turtle nests and don't let anyone disturb them.'

Carefully, she copied the words onto the big poster sheet, and in the middle, using the crayons she'd brought with her from Nairobi, she drew a big turtle swimming in the sea, just like the one she'd seen on the reef.

She worked at her picture for a long time, and when it was finished she sat back and looked at it. She was satisfied. It was one of the best things she'd ever done.

She wanted to run off at once and take it to Grace's office, but it was nearly the hottest part of the day now, and she didn't feel like going out into the sun. Instead, she pulled another sheet of paper towards her and began to doodle.

Figures rolled onto the paper under her pencil. There was Joseph, with his long slim legs and white shorts, kicking a football, and their best friend, Tom, in Nairobi, with his thatch of blond hair and freckly nose, and Sarah, her foster-mother, waving a towel as she ran out to her vegetable patch to chase some baboons away from her beans. And now here was Prof, his battered old hat resting on his unruly hair, peering down at a pile of stones on the ground. A long way away from him, on the far edge of the paper, was Minette, her long hair dragged back to the nape of her neck, a long lead from her hand pulling at a grotesquely elongated sausage dog. Minette's eyes were crossed, her tongue stuck out and her dress was savagely ripped up the front. As an afterthought, Afra drew a witch's hat on her head and a bubble coming out of her mouth in which she wrote, 'I am a witch.'

Tired, she put her pencil down. It really was very hot now, and she was thirsty. It must be nearly time for tea. Surely the others would be back soon? She went out of the dining room to the kitchen to ask for a cool drink from the fridge. There was no one in there, so she helped herself to a glass of water from the filter.

She finished her drink, put her glass down and went back to the dining room. Prof, Joseph and Minette had come back. They were looking at the drawings she had done. Prof and Joseph were admiring the poster, but Minette was looking at the doodles.

'Hey, Afra,' said Prof, seeing her by the door. 'You have been busy. This is beautiful.'

Without answering, Afra ran up and snatched the doodles off the table. She looked up at

Minette, expecting to see a satisfying flame of anger in her eyes. Instead she saw a stricken look.

I've hurt her, thought Afra.

She waited for a sense of triumph. It didn't come. Instead, she felt a small shadow of regret.

11

HANI DISGRACES HIMSELF

It rained in the night. Huge drops the size of peas splattered down onto the tin roof of Afra's little cabin, waking her up. She lay and listened for a while to the drumming sound it made, wondering if the glass of her window would stand up to the battering of the bougainvillea branches that were being hurled against it by the wild wind, but her bed was warm and comfortable and she drifted off again into sleep.

In the morning, leaves and twigs lay everywhere, torn off the bushes and trees, and Mr Mohammed was muttering to himself as he swept the debris off his gravel paths. But there was a fresh smell in the air and even the sky, cloudless once again, looked as if it had been washed clean.

Afra went to the edge of the compound and looked down towards the beach. Joseph came up behind her.

'You missed breakfast,' he said.

'What? What's the time?'

'Ten o'clock.'

'I didn't realize. I slept in. Did you hear the storm?'

He grinned.

'Not until a coconut fell onto the roof of my room. It was like a gun. I thought someone was shooting at me. I nearly died of fright.'

She looked back towards the main building.

'Where's Prof?'

Joseph looked awkward.

'He went out.'

She snorted.

'He went to the hotel, I bet, to see her. He's gone crazy. I think it's just disgusting.'

'It's not! You're so unfair, Afra. You don't—'

'Joseph.' She turned on him furiously. 'Don't say a word, OK? Not a word.'

He put up his hands and backed away from her, as if he was placating a lunatic with a gun.

'OK. I'm sorry. Take it easy, OK?'

She tried to laugh.

'Oh wow, you look quite scared.'

He shook his head.

'That's because you are a scary person.'

She thought about this.

'I'm not really. You know I'm not. It's just that I'm so mad with him, I feel kind of crazy about everything.'

'You don't have to tell me,' Joseph said with feeling. 'I had noticed.'

'You'd feel the same,' Afra flashed back, 'if Sarah found herself a boyfriend.'

They both tried to conjure up the idea of

Joseph's large, comfortable mother with a boyfriend. They caught each other's eyes and laughed, then Afra put up her hand and Joseph slapped it.

'I'm going down to the beach,' Joseph said. 'The waves are so big after the storm last night. Maybe they have washed up some interesting things.'

Afra followed him down the steps.

A small figure was walking along the shore towards them, his head down, as if he was looking for something.

'Hussein!' shouted Joseph, cupping his mouth with his hands.

The crash of the rollers, pounding onto the hard sand, drowned his voice, but a moment later Hussein looked up, saw Afra and Joseph and ran towards them.

'What have you found?' Joseph looked curiously at a white plastic stick Hussein was holding.

Hussein tapped the stick angrily on his left palm.

'This? It's from a trawler. It's a light stick. They use them to attract the fish into their nets.'

'What are you going to do with it? Does it still work?' Like the others, Afra had slipped into speaking in Swahili.

'No, it doesn't work, and I'm going to smash it up,' said Hussein savagely. 'And I wish I could smash up the trawlers.'

No one said anything for a moment.

'You didn't go fishing today?' Joseph said at last.

'No.' Hussein shook his head. 'The sea was too rough this morning, but my father is going out this afternoon. I will go with him.'

'I wish we could go with you,' said Afra.

Hussein looked at her, surprised.

'Really? You would really like to come? But you would have to work, and help us.'

'I'd like that.' Afra hadn't thought about it before, but now she realized that a trip out to sea in Hussein's outrigger was exactly what she wanted. It would make up for yesterday's missed outing in the glass-bottomed boat, and it would take her far out of reach of Prof and Minette.

'I'll ask my father,' Hussein said eagerly. 'It would be fun. I'd show you everything we do out there.'

'And we'd better ask Prof,' Joseph said.

Afra tossed her head.

'I don't care if he likes it or not,' she said. 'He can jump in the sea and get eaten by an octopus for all I care.'

Hussein shook his head.

'Octopuses don't eat people,' he said. 'You are thinking of sharks.'

'No, I'm not. An octopus would be better,' said Afra with relish. 'Imagine all those suckers all over you. You'd want to die. It would be much nastier than sharks.'

Joseph wasn't listening. An anxious crease had appeared between his brows.

'We have to ask him, Afra. You know that.'

'You can ask him now,' Hussein said, pointing down the beach. 'He is coming.'

Afra turned. Prof and Minette, who was wearing her scarlet dress again, were walking towards them across the rain-flattened sand. Joseph shot a glance at Afra, but she had turned her head away.

'Hussein says we can go out fishing with his father,' Joseph blurted out, as soon as Prof and Minette were within earshot.

Prof looked down at Hussein.

'That's very kind,' he said, 'but—'

'And I'm going,' Afra said rudely, 'whether you say I can or not.'

Prof scowled.

'Afra—'

'*Vraiment*?' interrupted Minette. 'You want to go out in one of those little fishing boats? Are they safe?'

'Of course they're safe!' said Afra scornfully, looking at Prof. 'Fishermen go out in them every day.'

'They are less safe, however,' Prof said drily, 'after a storm, when there is a heavy swell. Not today, Afra. Tomorrow, perhaps, if the sea is calm.'

'That's it. That's it!' Afra's fists were balled and

her eyes stormy. 'You never, never let me do what I—!'

A shout from Joseph interrupted her in mid-flow.

'Hani! No!' he yelled, dashing off up the beach.

It took Afra a few seconds to realize what was happening, and when she did she was momentarily unable to move. Hani had discovered the turtle's nest. He was scrabbling at it with feverish enthusiasm, his forepaws digging so fast they'd almost become an invisible blur, his sharp tail quivering with excitement.

Afra came to her senses and took off after Joseph, her feet flying across the sand. Joseph, almost at the nest, tripped over a piece of drift-wood and fell sprawling into a pile of dried seaweed. Afra leaped over him, reached Hani, and snatching at his collar, hauled him away from the nest. The little dog squirmed and yapped, outraged at the indignity, and Afra had to overcome an impulse to hit him.

Minette came running up and scooped Hani up into her arms. She glared at Afra over her wriggling bundle.

'What's the matter with you? He didn't do anything wrong. He likes digging out crabs, you know he does.'

'Didn't do anything wrong? He likes digging out crabs?' A red tide of anger was rising in Afra, and she gave into it luxuriously. 'Don't you understand, you stupid cow, that the turtle's nest is right there? No, you don't. You don't know anything. You don't care about anything. It's just fine by you if he digs up the eggs. It's no problem if that turtle mother's work was wasted. Who cares if turtles become extinct anyway? You don't think about anyone except yourself and your greedy, stupid, horrible little dog. You think you can do whatever you like, have whatever you want, take—'

She felt a stinging slap on her arm and turned round. Prof was lowering his hand, his eyes blazing with an anger she had never seen in them before.

She felt almost faint with shock.

'You hit me!' she whispered.

'Stop that. Stop it at once!' Prof was shouting, his face red. 'How dare you! Apologize to Minette!'

'Apologize? For telling the truth?' she screamed back at him. 'I'd rather die.'

They stood glaring at each other. Prof was tensed as if he might hit her again, while Afra stood her ground, as if she was daring him to.

Joseph made them both drop their eyes. He had got down on his knees and was investigating the hole that Hani had dug.

'Hani wasn't going for the turtles,' he said, looking from one to the other placatingly. 'The middle of the nest is further up the bank. He really was just trying to dig out another crab.'

Afra stamped her foot.

'I hate you! I hate you all!' she sobbed, and turning round, she raced away along the beach, not caring where she was going.

12

OUTRIGGER

Afra stopped running at last and dropped down onto the sand. She was hot, thirsty and full of self-pity. She'd stubbed her toe, too, unprotected as it was by her open sandal, on a stone, and waves of pain coursed up her leg.

She sat still for a moment, unable to move.

He hit me, she kept thinking.

As far as she could remember, her father had never hit her before. She was torn between outrage and a kind of fierce satisfaction.

He'll have to be sorry for that, she thought.

Something caught the corner of her eye and she looked up. Joseph was splashing along through the shallow water at the sea's edge, letting the wavelets suck around his feet. He looked up at her, as if he was deciding whether to approach her or not.

He's disgusted with me, thought Afra. Her mood changed at once. Her anger turned into dismay as she saw herself through his eyes.

She lifted her hand and gave him a tentative wave. At once he came up the beach and sat beside her.

'Afra, why were you so—' he began.

'I couldn't help it. She's just so—' she said at the same time.

They looked unsmilingly at each other.

'There's no point in talking about it,' said Afra, 'is there?'

Joseph wriggled his bare feet in the sand.

'Not really. Just don't try to pull me into it, that's all. Into a fight with you and Prof, I mean.'

She frowned.

'You are in it. You're practically my brother.'

'Yes, but Prof's not my father, and I don't care about him and Minette. In fact,' he took a deep breath and looked her bravely in the eye, 'I like her.'

'You *like* her?' she said, revolted. Then she stopped. 'Maybe I would if she didn't have her hooks into my father,' she went on, making a heroic effort to be fair. 'But the way it is, I just think she's a—'

She caught his eye and stopped.

'What are we going to do now?' he said, after a pause.

She looked up at him, frowning.

'I'm not going back to them, if that's what you think. I'm not crawling back there to say sorry.'

He sighed.

'I know that. I'm not a fool. I'm not going to persuade you. It would be impossible anyway.'

She managed to laugh.

'I couldn't walk that far anyway. I mashed my toe on a stone back there.'

He bent over to look at it.

'I can't see anything.'

'No. It's only bruised.' She wriggled it. 'It doesn't feel so bad now. The pain's gone off a bit.' She looked up. 'I guess I'll just be able to walk as far as the village. Where's Hussein?'

'He ran off before you started shouting at Minette. Didn't you see him go?'

'No.'

She was looking speculatively at the big rock beyond which the fishermen kept their canoes and nets.

'I'm going to find him,' she said, making a sudden decision and getting to her feet.

'Find Hussein? Why?' Joseph jumped up too.

'So he can take me out fishing,' said Afra with determination, beginning to limp along the beach.

'Afra, are you crazy? You can't! It's not safe in this weather. Look, none of the boats have gone out today.'

'Oh? What's that then?'

She pointed ahead. Four or five men had appeared from behind the rock. They were carrying a heavy dugout canoe down the beach to the water's edge while the smaller figure of Hussein trotted along beside them. Afra speeded up. She was almost running now, in spite of her sore toe. Joseph ran beside her.

'Don't do this, Afra,' he pleaded. 'It will give us more trouble. More shouting. I've had enough of it.'

She stopped and spun round at him, her anger boiling up again.

'Go back then,' she snarled. 'Go and make eyes at sweet, darling Minette, and show Prof what a good boy you are.'

'That's unfair,' he said angrily. 'You're mean.'

He began to walk away. She watched him go, feeling a little ashamed of herself, then she heard Hussein calling to her. She limped quickly up to him.

'Did you ask your father?' she asked him. 'Can I go out with you?'

She almost didn't want to any more, but pride was pushing her to go through with it.

Hussein looked at her, surprised.

'Yes, my father says you can come, but your own father told you it was too dangerous.'

'Oh, he changed his mind,' she said glibly. 'Joseph came to tell me. He says it's fine if I go.'

'But Joseph isn't coming?'

She looked round to see Joseph standing watching, a little way away. Something about his irresolute posture maddened her again.

'He doesn't dare come,' she said, raising her voice. 'He's chicken.'

'Chicken?' Hussein looked puzzled.

'Scared. He's too scared,' she said, speaking even louder.

She could see even from this distance that Joseph's face was stiff with anger. He galloped up to her, grabbed her by the arms and shook her.

'Don't try playing tricks on me,' he said. 'That's a horrible way to get at me. I will come with you, but only for one reason. I know how you are when you are in this bad mood. You do stupid things. You get into a worse mess. I'm coming only to see that you're OK. Do you understand that, Afra?'

She looked away.

'OK. I'm sorry. I guess saying that was kind of low.'

'Yes, it was low. And you have to promise me—'

'Promise what?'

He dropped his hands.

'Nothing. What would be the point? It is stupid to ask you. I wanted you to promise not to lose your temper again, and not to do anything crazy, but I might as well ask a – a bird to promise not to fly.'

She buffeted him lightly on the chest.

'I'll try, OK? That's a promise. The best I can do. And thanks.'

'Thanks? What for?'

'Oh, I don't know. Everything.'

The canoe was in the water now. Hussein and

his father were setting up the outrigging, the system of spars and floats on either side of the canoe that would act as stabilizers on a rough sea, and prevent the little craft from capsizing. The other four men ran back up behind the big rock to fetch a second canoe.

'Can we help?' Afra said, nervously addressing Hussein's father. She had realized that Prof might come to find her, and wanted to get out to sea before he appeared.

'You don't know how to do this,' Hussein said. He was working beside Abu Bekir, his father, a short man, who wore an old straw hat on his head, its drooping tattered brim shading his weather-beaten, deeply lined face. He had said nothing so far, merely grunting out the occasional command and sending Hussein splashing round to the far side of the canoe.

The boat was ready at last. Abu Bekir walked out through the long reach of shallow water that separated the shore from the deep water, towing the canoe behind him towards the place where the seabed dropped suddenly away to a much greater depth. Afra and Joseph walked along behind, close to Hussein who was pushing the canoe from the stern. The sun burned down on Afra's head, in spite of the hat she was wearing, and the light dancing on the water dazzled her eyes. Little fish darted round her ankles, and sponges brushed her feet. She had to watch out in case she trod on the dark poisoned spikes of a sea urchin, or stumbled into a hollow on the rocky bed.

They reached the deep water at last.

'Get in,' said Hussein, steadying the boat so that Afra and Joseph could scramble on board. He climbed in lightly after them, his father following him.

The canoe was long and narrow. It had been hollowed out of a single tree trunk, and the wood was bleached and worn with age. A short mast held a triangular sail aloft, and in the bottom of the boat lay a neatly folded fishing net with floats stitched into it, a bucket, a couple of long poles and a flat basket in which to keep the catch.

It was rougher now. Only ripples had disturbed the shallows, but here there was a real swell. Afra looked anxiously at the frail craft and tried to suppress the thought that Prof might have been right after all. Maybe this was a mad idea. Maybe the little boat would turn over and sink in the heavier seas out beyond the shore.

It was too late now. The sail was up and the rigging tightened. Abu Bekir grabbed one of the long poles and pushed against the side of the underwater shelf to thrust the boat away from the shallows. Then the waves picked them up and they were away, bobbing up and down like a cork on a bowl of shaken water.

Looking back, Afra could see four other canoes

following behind, their little tan-coloured sails rising and falling as they breasted the swell.

'Here,' Abu Bekir said at last. He had hardly spoken a word, communicating only with nods of the head and a few expressive grunts, and he indicated wordlessly that it was time to lower the nets and start fishing. Hussein moved quickly, lifting the net out from under Afra's and Joseph's legs and handing one end of it to his father. They were concentrating closely on what they were doing, taking care to keep the net from tangling in the floats. They lowered it at last into the water.

'How do you know where to fish?' Joseph asked curiously.

'My father, he knows the sea,' Hussein said proudly. 'He knows the fish.'

Afra looked over the edge of the canoe and gazed down into the water. She had to be careful not to lean too far as the little craft had no keel and, in spite of the outrigging, was inclined to list easily to one side. She couldn't see anything at first through the sparkling light glancing off the fractured surface of the sea, so she looked over the other side. In the shadow cast by the canoe she could see straight into the depths below.

Some way down (she couldn't tell how far) was the white sandy seabed, darkened in places by patches of weed and outcrops of rock. Only a few small fish, too small to be bothered by the wide mesh of the net, were swimming with the current.

This was a different underwater world from the bright, richly inhabited reef where she had snorkelled yesterday. It was wilder, stranger, emptier and more dangerous. It suited her changing moods. She was almost sorry now that the waves were not higher and the rocks below more jagged.

If I drowned he'd be sorry, she thought. I almost hope I do.

Then Joseph's foot brushed against her leg.

But then I suppose everyone else would drown too, she thought guiltily.

'I didn't really mean it,' she whispered inaudibly.

'Over there! Look!' Joseph said. 'Something's floating on the surface.'

She looked up. Some distance away, floating towards them, was a confused mass of brown, white and blue stuff, bobbing about on the surface of the waves.

Hussein drew in his breath and said something excitedly to his father, who laughed and shook his head.

'What did you think it was?' asked Afra.

'There are strange creatures in the sea,' Hussein said seriously. 'My grandfather has told me about them. From the waist down they are fishes. From the waist upwards they are people.'

'Mermaids!' exclaimed Afra. 'But they're not real.'

'They are!' objected Hussein. 'They are

spirits. They don't come near the shore. Out there in the deep ocean—' he waved his arm towards the open sea, 'that's where they live.'

'Those are just stories,' Joseph said. 'I don't believe in them.'

'You don't believe in them because you have never seen them,' Hussein said simply, 'but my grandfather told me. He knows they are there.'

Afra shivered. Today, nothing seemed real. Things she had thought would always be there were safe no longer. Prof, she had always believed, would remain true to his dead wife. She and her father, she had never doubted, would be a twosome for ever more, with nothing added and nothing taken away.

If she had misunderstood that reality, what else might she have mistaken? Why shouldn't there be mermaids out there in the ocean? Why should Hussein and his father both be wrong?

The strange object had floated closer to them. Afra could see now that it was a bundle of coarsely woven nylon sacking twisted round a mass of knotted blue rope.

Something else was tangled in the rope, something smooth and curved and rounded. It was a shell. And from the front of the shell rose a little beaked head and two feebly waving flippers, trying in vain to free themselves.

'A turtle!' cried Afra. 'Look! It's a turtle!'

13

A BATTLE AT SEA

Hussein's father, balancing himself skilfully in the narrow canoe, pushed the children out of the way and reached down into the matted bundle of flotsam with his knife. A moment later he had slashed through the cords and sacking, and had lifted the turtle clear. He put it in the bucket.

It was a young one, its shell no more than 30 cm long. The brown and gold markings on its lustrous domed carapace glistened, but its eyes were dull and its flippers moved only feebly.

'We should put it back into the sea right now,' Afra said impatiently, 'before it gets more distressed.'

Abu Bekir was busy with the mass of ropes and sacking, pushing them away from the side of the canoe in case they tangled with his net, and he didn't answer.

'It will only get caught again,' Hussein said, 'in our net, or the others behind us. Anyway, my father will get money for it.'

'Money? You'll sell it?'

Afra's voice came out on a rising squeak.

Joseph glared at her and gave her a powerful nudge.

'Who will buy it?' he asked Hussein, keeping a stern eye on the fuming Afra.

'Nobody buys it,' Hussein answered. 'Mrs Otieno, she will give my father money when he takes the turtle to her.'

'Mrs Otieno? Why?' Afra had subsided, but she was still frowning.

'She will measure him, check his health, I don't know,' Hussein said. 'Maybe she will put a tag on him before she lets him go back into the ocean. He is a hawksbill, the rarest kind. She will be very pleased, I think.'

'Are they doing a study, then?' asked Joseph, looking interested. 'My Uncle Titus works for KWS. He does things like that.'

'A study? I don't know. But the tags tell things. If you catch a turtle with a tag, you can see where it came from. They travel so far! You would not believe it.'

The three of them looked down respectfully at the creature in the bucket, holding on to the narrow sides of the rocking canoe to steady themselves. Sharp points made an elegant edge to its carapace, and black scales fringed with white covered its strongly beaked head. It looked up suddenly, and Afra could see that its throat was the colour of thick cream. It was puckered like the skin of a chicken.

'His flipper is hurt. Look,' she said.

Gently, she picked up the turtle's front left flipper and examined it. It was surprisingly dry and frail to the touch, and almost as thin as paper. It spread out on her hand like a fan, and she could see a tear in it, where a piece of twine had dug deep during the turtle's struggle to free itself.

The turtle objected to being handled. It puffed out its gorge and made a feeble squeaking hiss.

'Sorry,' said Afra. 'I only wanted to know if you needed first aid. I guess you don't. Anyway, salt water's best for cuts, and you'll get plenty of that when you're back home.'

She let the flipper go. The turtle shifted awkwardly, then subsided, seeming to resign itself to whatever fate might befall it.

Abu Bekir had poled the mass of flotsam well away from the canoe now. He turned to check the net and gave a sharp exclamation.

Hussein looked up, shading his eyes, and stared intently along the coast towards the south. Afra tried to see what he was looking at, but there was only another pair of outrigger canoes, their occupants sitting peacefully in the bows, waiting no doubt for their nets to do their work.

'What's the matter?' she asked Hussein, only mildly interested.

'Those boats, they are not from our village,' Hussein said, puckering his eyes as he strained to see better. He said something in Kivumba to his father, then reverted back to Swahili. 'That one near to us, and the other behind it, I have never seen them before. The men are strangers.'

'They come from the next village I suppose,' said Afra, switching her attention back to the turtle, whose lids had closed and were meeting, bird-like, across the middle of its eyes.

A quality of intent stillness in the others made her look up again. An old motor boat, with a mast and a sail and a battered prow lifted high up out of the water, was coming out fast from behind the nearest headland. She could hear the urgent stutter of its engine and the swish of water against its bows.

At the sight of the motor boat, the men in the two strange canoes leaped into rapid action. They waved to it, and seemed to exchange some kind of signal. Then Afra, who was watching one of the men standing in the stern of the motor boat, saw him pick up a stick-like thing, the length and thickness of a candle, tug a string that hung from it, and throw it into the water. At once an explosion cracked out, shattering the peace of the drowsy afternoon. The bang made her ears sing, and a plume of water rose into the air.

'Dynamiters!' roared Abu Bekir. 'Thieves!'

He was pulling in his net with the speed and energy of three men. Hussein, needing no command, was yanking up the other end of it, bundling it as fast as he could into the canoe.

Afra's heart pounded, and she was flooded with a panic so intense she had to hold herself back from leaping into the sea and swimming for the shore. Before she could move, the fishing net that Hussein and his father were hauling in landed on top of her. She saw that it was covering the bucket too, threatening to tip it over and entangle the turtle again. She lunged forward and managed to pull it free, then sank back onto the floor of the canoe, hugging the bucket in her arms. The canoe tilted alarmingly, and for a moment she was afraid it would capsize.

Joseph was helping Hussein to drag in the last length of net. Abu Bekir was in the stern of the canoe, shouting and gesticulating to the other village fishermen, who were paddling towards him as fast as they could.

The results of the explosion were already horrifyingly evident. Every living creature that had a few minutes before been swimming through the water, or nosing along the seabed, or grazing on the weed-covered rocks, was now coming up to float, dead, on the surface of the sea. Fish, eels, squid, octopuses, stingrays – all lay lifeless, their pale bellies glistening, their eyes clouded with death, their fins and tails drooping and still.

Afra could see now that a net was suspended between the two strange canoes. With practised speed, their occupants were paddling furiously, dragging the net between them to scoop up the harvest of dead fish.

The other two village canoes, each manned with two men, had reached Hussein's father now. Their crews' faces were suffused with anger, and they were yelling furiously at the strangers.

'Hussein, what's happening?' Afra called out. 'What are they going to do?'

Her first panic had subsided and a feeling of unreality had taken its place.

Hussein didn't answer, but Joseph, who was gripping the sides of the canoe so hard that the muscles of his arms bulged out, said, 'There's going to be a fight.'

'A fight? They can't!' gasped Afra. 'Those guys have that big motor boat, and there are at least three of them on it, and their two canoes, and we only have our four little boats. Anyway, these little boats are so wobbly we'll all end up in the sea!'

But she knew that Joseph was right. The air was charged with hostility. Hussein's father had flung his hat down and grabbed one of the long punting poles. He was kneeling up, balancing the pole in his hands and shouting instructions to Hussein, who was paddling as fast as he could towards the motor boat through the choppy sea.

This isn't happening, thought Afra. It's a dream or something.

She was holding onto the bucket with all her

strength, clutching at it, her arms strained, as if the turtle inside it was a talisman, her only hope of safety.

The other villagers were paddling frantically towards the two strange canoes, yelling at their occupants, who were working as fast as they could, trying to haul in their catch and get it up onto the motor boat and away down the coast before the others could catch up with them. But the villagers were close to them now.

'What are they doing?' Afra shouted to Joseph. 'I can't see.'

'They're going for the net,' Joseph called back. 'They're going to try to cut the net!'

The two other village fishing teams had reached the dynamiters' net now and they were hacking at it with their knives. The men on the motor boat were leaning over the side, shouting threateningly and shaking their fists.

The gap between Hussein's father's boat and the motor boat was closing rapidly. Afra watched the big boat's dark sides approach with terror. The men on it were so close she could read the expressions on their faces. They looked violent and desperate. Their thin limbs showed through their ragged clothes and they looked down on the village fishermen with rage and contempt.

Afra wanted to shake Hussein's father, and shout in his ear, 'Go back! Get away! They've got dynamite! They could blow us all up!' but she didn't dare move from her place in the bows of the canoe.

The villagers were hacking at the dynamiters' net now, sawing at it with violent thrusts of their knives. Afra looked up at the motor boat. One of the men had run away from the rail and he was racing back, sliding on the dirty wet deck. He came back shouting, holding out something to show the frenzied men cutting the net below. Afra saw, with a terrified lurch of her stomach, that it was a stick of dynamite.

'No!' she screamed, half struggling to her feet so that the canoe rocked violently. 'Don't throw it!'

The net-cutters looked up, saw the stick of dynamite in their enemy's hand and, with fear in their eyes, left their task and began to paddle backwards away from the net.

Hussein's father, though, seemed maddened with rage. He had steered his canoe right alongside the motor boat, and was lashing out with his pole, trying to hit the men on the deck above him.

He can't do that! Afra thought with disbelief. He can't take them on alone!

Abu Bekir landed a hit on one of the men's legs. The man turned towards him with a snarl, grabbed the end of the pole and tried to wrestle it out of Abu Bekir's hands. The canoe rocked violently, and the spars lashing the outer buoys to it creaked alarmingly, threatening to come loose.

The man above gave up suddenly, and Abu Bekir lost his balance and fell backwards. He landed heavily, knocking the bucket half out of Afra's arms. She lurched sideways, and managed to retain her hold on it, but at that moment a roar of triumph went up. The two other village fishermen, while everyone's attention had been fixed on Abu Bekir and the men on the motor boat, had sneaked back to the net, and had succeeded in cutting it loose. It was floating away on the current, its burden of dead fish drifting free again.

Afra didn't see it. Her eyes were fixed on the man above. Infuriated by the loss of the fish, he had pulled the tape on his stick of dynamite and sent it curving up into the air. It landed in the water only twenty metres from Abu Bekir's canoe. She heard the roar and crack, and had time to see, as if in slow motion, the great fountain of water spurt up into the air. Then something hit her on the side of her head. She toppled sideways over the edge of the canoe into the sea, and lost consciousness.

14

THE TURTLE IS RELEASED

Afra's faint lasted no more than a few seconds. She came round as Abu Bekir's sinewy hands hauled her back into the canoe, and she lay on the bottom, too dazzled by the sun to open her eyes, afraid, in any case, to see what might be happening.

There were confused voices all around her, and someone was splashing water onto her face. She flinched and opened her eyes.

'What happened?' she said weakly.

'Hussein's father hit you by mistake with the end of his pole,' Joseph said. 'I guess he knocked you out.'

Afra shut her eyes and opened them again. A circle of concerned faces was looking down at her. Joseph was closest. He saw that the sun was in her eyes and shaded them with her hat, which someone must have retrieved from the water and wrung out. Behind him was Abu Bekir, on whose normally reserved face was a look of deep anxiety, with Hussein peering round his elbow. The canoe was still bobbing close up against the motor boat, and the men on board were looking down at her. Even in their faces she could see shock and concern.

Who are they? Why are they here? Afra thought muzzily. Then she remembered what had happened, and realized at the same time that the noise of their engine had stopped.

She began to struggle to sit up, and the momentary unnatural silence was broken. The men on the motor boat began to argue with each other, sounding so furious that it seemed as if they would start fighting on their own deck. Afra caught a few words of their strange dialect of Swahili.

'Fool! You could have—'

'Don't you know what happens if we hurt someone?'

'She's a tourist or something. You know what trouble that—'

'Get the engine going! We have to get out of here!'

The other two canoes from the village had paddled up to Abu Bekir.

'Is she all right?' one of the men said, looking at Afra but addressing Abu Bekir.

'Yes, thank God,' Abu Bekir said.

He turned and smiled at Afra, and the anxiety on his rugged face melted into kindly concern.

'You are all right, aren't you?' he said diffidently. 'It was an accident. The pole – it slipped in my hand and hit your head.'

'It's OK. I'm fine,' said Afra.

She tried sitting up, and lay back again. She felt a shameful desire to cry, and knew that if she started she wouldn't be able to stop.

One of the men on the motor boat, who wore a rough bandage on his arm, called out tentatively, 'Is the little girl all right?'

Abu Bekir spat contemptuously over the side of his canoe.

'How do I know? And if she is, it's no thanks to you, you murdering thieves.'

'Hey!' the bandaged man objected. 'You are the one who hit her. What are you doing, bringing tourist kids out here anyway, you old fool?'

Abu Bekir grunted furiously, and began to lurch to his feet again, and for a moment it seemed as if another fight would break out, but one of the village men said soothingly to Abu Bekir, 'Leave it. We've done enough,' and someone on the motor boat elbowed the bandaged man out of the way and said, 'Listen, brother, we didn't mean anyone to get hurt. We're poor men. Our kids are hungry. We only wanted some fish.'

'Go somewhere else for your fish!' Abu Bekir called up angrily. 'Don't come and dynamite ours. You've killed everything here!'

'The trawlers have taken all the fish near our village,' the bandaged man said. 'There's nothing left for us.'

There was a short silence, then Abu Bekir

shouted, 'We'll fight you again if you come back. What are you waiting for? Get out of here!'

'We can't,' the other man called out. 'Our engine has broken down and the wind is against us. Be merciful, brothers. We are in your hands. We promise we will never come here again.'

The village men began to laugh.

'Your engine's broken down? We've got you now!' they called out. 'Come back to our village! We'll give you something you won't forget. Something worse than a broken-down engine!'

Afra was feeling a little stronger, though her head was aching badly. She tried sitting up again. She could hear in the distance the sound of a motor boat coming nearer. The others had heard it too.

'Here comes the KWS boat!' Abu Bekir shouted gleefully. 'Now you're in for it!'

The men on the motor boat were clustering round their engine, trying desperately to get it started. There were eight of them on board now, as far as Afra could see. The crews from the two canoes had dismantled their outrigging, lashed their canoes to the back of the motor boat, and scrambled on board. They were looking anxiously towards the KWS's little white launch, which was rapidly approaching.

Afra felt a dreadful sinking in her stomach, which had nothing to do with the bang on her head.

'Is Prof there?' she asked Joseph. 'Can you see him?'

He had to screw his eyes up against the sun as he watched the motor boat approach.

'No, I can't see him.' She could tell by his voice that he was relieved too. 'I can only see Mrs Otieno and one – no, two rangers. Yes, Abel and Massoud. Abel's driving the boat.'

The turtle, which had been lying quietly in the bucket, suddenly began to move about, scrabbling at the smooth plastic sides.

'At least we saved you,' Afra said, looking down gloomily at the little creature. 'If you'd been in the water when the dynamite went off, you'd be feeling kind of sick now, I guess.'

'He would be dead,' said Hussein, looking at the turtle too. 'It's very, very dangerous if you are in the water. The explosion kind of melts you from inside. I found a turtle once, after the dynamiters came. The shell was OK. Just normal. But inside it the meat was like it had been cooked. It was a sort of mush.'

'That's so horrible.' Afra shuddered. She stroked the turtle's shell gently with her forefinger. 'Poor little guy. You won't forget this in a hurry.'

'How do you know?' Joseph objected. 'How do you know turtles have memories?'

'They must have, dumbo,' said Afra, who was feeling a little stronger, 'or how would they find their way home to lay their eggs when they've swum halfway round the world?'

The KWS launch was almost within calling distance, and Abu Bekir had begun shouting to it already.

'They are here, look! The dynamiters! Two sticks they let off! They almost blew us to bits!'

Afra could see Grace now. Her unruly hair had escaped from its pins and was flying wildly round her head. She was wearing a blue kanga, a cloth wrapped sarong-like round her middle, and her T-shirt was stretched round her ample shoulders. From a distance she looked comfortable and motherly, but close-up her face was uncompromisingly stern.

She ignored Abu Bekir and the village fishermen and waited till the KWS launch was directly alongside the motor boat. Then, with an ungainly scramble, she hoisted herself up onto its deck, Massoud following in her wake.

The village men below watched and waited, straining their ears to hear what was happening.

'Lock them all up!' one of them shouted.

'Give them over to us! We'll show them!' called out another.

Grace ignored them. Afra, watching curiously, saw the men on the boat cringing as she spoke to them. They were shifting their feet nervously and twisting their hands together, but the noise of the KWS launch's engine drowned their voices.

At last Grace finished, and climbed back down into the launch. She looked down into Abu Bekir's canoe, to Afra and Joseph, for the first time.

'You had better come with me,' she said. 'Eh, Afra, your father is a worried man.'

Afra looked up at her, her face set.

'Why? Does he know I'm here?'

'He knows. He went to the village and someone there told him they had seen you go out with the boats.' She stopped and looked at Afra more closely. 'You look pale. Well, not pale, more yellow, or green even. And your clothes are wet. What happened?'

'She hit her head,' Joseph said hastily. 'She fell into the sea. It wasn't anybody's fault.'

'I'm fine,' Afra said hastily, not wanting to make trouble for Abu Bekir. 'Nothing happened, really. I just got wet, that's all.'

'It was the thieves' fault,' said Hussein, looking anxiously from Grace to his father. 'They were stealing our fish. Are you going to arrest them?'

Grace was leaning out of the launch to hang onto Afra, who was trying to stand up. She was wobbling dangerously, making the canoe rock beneath her.

'No, I won't arrest them,' Grace said. 'But they will be summoned. They will have to go to court. They will be fined and I think they will lose their boats.'

Afra, stepping up into the launch from the

bows of the canoe, almost missed her footing and fell back into the sea, but at the last moment she managed to scramble on board. She groped her way to the bench that ran round the well in the stern of the boat and sank down onto it.

She looked up and saw three of the men on the motor boat staring down at her. She could hardly bear to meet their eyes.

They're going to lose their boats, she thought. How are they going to live?

The other sailors were trying to fix up the sail, so that they could start their long slow journey home. Their faces were blank with misery. Embarrassed, she looked beyond them, far out to sea, and saw, for the first time, the ghostly grey line of trawlers. They seemed to be hanging, mirage-like, in the sky, above the surface of the water, far out of reach of the men whose lives they had ruined.

Joseph had climbed onto the launch in Afra's wake.

'What about the turtle?' she asked him.

He pointed back into the canoe. Abu Bekir was holding out the bucket and was showing the little hawksbill to Grace. She leant over and took it from him, then picked it up to examine it. The turtle worked its flippers vigorously through the air as if it was trying to swim. Afra could see its undershell for the first time. It was a yellowish white, like its neck, and was deeply grooved with a pattern like the veins on a leaf.

Grace put the turtle back in the bucket.

'Are you going to take him back with us?' Afra asked.

She shook her head.

'No. He has been stressed too much already. We will release him now. Take him, Joseph. Put him back in the sea.'

Pleased, Joseph took the turtle carefully out of the bucket again and carried it to the side of the launch. Afra watched enviously. She would have liked to hold the little creature herself, to feel his weight in her hands, to be the one to release him.

But I touched him, she thought, remembering the feel of the turtle's smooth gleaming shell under her fingertip and the softness of its flipper in her palm. No one has the right to more.

She leaned over the side to watch as Joseph lowered the turtle gently into the water.

'He will go off like a rocket,' Grace said. 'You will see.'

But the turtle didn't. When Joseph had released it, it seemed to hesitate for a moment, as if finding its strength again. Then it worked one flipper tentatively and at last, seeming to realize that it was really free, it scooped confidently at the water with its right foreflipper, keeling over to the side as it did so, and with a deft thrust, righted itself and was away.

For a moment, Afra saw it still, a dark shadow in the water, then it was gone.

She felt flat, as if a friend had gone away for ever.

That's dumb, she thought. I should be glad. He's home now.

Grace was talking to Abu Bekir. She reached under her kanga into a pocket of the trousers concealed underneath, and pulled out a screw of knotted cloth. She untied it, and counted some coins into Abu Bekir's hands. He smiled, and stowed them carefully in the bow of the canoe.

The other villagers were working with their nets, pulling in the dead fish that still floated on the surface of the sea, while the men on the motor boat looked on sourly. Grace watched them, her face sad, as Abel backed the launch away, then turned it and began to drive full steam ahead for the shore.

'At least they'll have something to take home tonight,' she said, 'even if the dynamiters have made the seabed here a desert for the next fifteen years.'

'Fifteen years?' gasped Joseph. 'You mean they won't be able to catch any fish for another fifteen years?'

'No, no.' Grace shook her head. 'It's only in an area of about fifty metres, where the dynamite went off, where everything, even the coral is dead. But they will fish beyond it tomorrow.'

Afra suddenly remembered something. She leaned out of the launch and called to Hussein and his father, 'Thank you! Thank you for taking us out. I'm sorry!'

She wasn't sure why she was apologizing, but somehow it seemed the right thing to do.

She sat back. The shore was rushing towards them now. They would be back at the KWS jetty in twenty minutes or less.

Her heart skipped a beat. Two figures were standing on the shore. Even at this distance, there was no mistaking that tall ungainly man with the old sunhat on his head, and the slim woman in the red dress who stood beside him. Prof and Minette were waiting on the beach.

15

A PAINFUL LANDING

Until the last few days, Afra had rarely felt the whip of her father's anger. He usually withdrew into coldness when he was annoyed. She could see, though, before the boat had reached the jetty, that he was in a white heat of rage. She started to feel sick and her legs trembled under her.

'Joseph,' she whispered, resisting the temptation to clutch at his hand, 'it's going to be a tough one. Oh boy, I'm sorry.'

He didn't answer, but she could sense the tension in him.

The boat was nosing up against the jetty. Afra wanted to hang back, to take cover behind Grace and the rangers, who were preparing to disembark as if nothing had happened, but she knew it would be pointless. She would have to face Prof sooner or later. She might as well get on with it.

She didn't look at him directly, but she could see out of the corner of her eye that he was standing as rigid as a block of wood, with his arms crossed over his chest. Minette, her dress blowing a little in the wind, seemed almost to flutter beside him.

Afra stepped out onto the jetty. Her head was aching violently, and the sick feeling had come back too. Behind her, she vaguely heard Grace and the rangers tie up the boat.

Grace called out, 'These kids, they are very lucky! There was a fight out there with the dynamiters. Afra got wet, but no harm was done. It is better, perhaps, to keep them away from the fishing boats. We never know when trouble is going to strike.' She seemed to read the expression on Prof's face. 'No harm is done,' she said again, then tactfully withdrew, following the rangers up the beach towards the KWS compound.

Afra forced herself to stand erect and walk up to her father.

He grabbed her arm and held it in a painful grip. His fingers were trembling.

'Afra, how could you? How could you? You did it deliberately, didn't you? You wanted me to be distraught with worry. Well, you certainly succeeded.'

She had been concentrating in order to stay on her feet, but faintness was engulfing her, creeping up her body in an irresistible tide. She sank down onto the sand and put her head between her knees. She could feel an odd pricking behind her eyes, but the faintness was receding. Somewhere miles above her head she heard Joseph say courageously, 'She was knocked out, Prof. There was a fight, and she got hit on the head by a pole.

She fell into the sea. I don't think she's feeling very well.'

There was a silence as Prof took this in, then, like a lion cheated of its prey, he turned on Joseph instead.

'As for you,' he said, spitting out the words, 'I thought I could trust you. Afra's totally irresponsible. Totally out of control. But you – I thought you at least had some sense. But out you go, against my express wishes, out to sea, in a crazy little boat, straight into a fight with dangerously armed men—'

'They weren't really armed, Prof,' Joseph interjected softly. 'They didn't have any guns.'

'Dynamite isn't a weapon, I suppose!' Prof rapped out scornfully. 'Don't argue with me, Joseph. I'm extremely disappointed in you.'

Afra lifted her head, making an effort to control the faintness that still threatened to engulf her.

'Prof, listen! It wasn't Joseph. He didn't want to come with me. I made him. It was all my fault.'

'That,' Prof said furiously, 'I can believe. It's always your fault. Well, I've had enough. You're going back to Nairobi tomorrow, the pair of you. On your own.'

Afra gasped.

'Please, Prof!' she pleaded. 'Don't! Don't send us away. Not Joseph, anyway. That's not fair. It's just not fair!'

She dropped her head again. To her astonishment, she sensed a swish of soft material and caught a waft of perfume as Minette bent down beside her and laid a cool hand on her forehead.

'Don't talk, *chérie*,' Minette said. 'Don't get upset.' She stood up again. 'Richard, listen to me. This child's half concussed. She needs peace and quiet and a darkened room. Stop shouting at them.'

'Stay out of this, please, Minette.' Prof sounded exasperated. 'Afra's behaviour to you has been absolutely disgraceful. I've never been so ashamed in my life. It's very nice of you to be so understanding, but it's not necessary. Afra can have a day in bed to get over her headache, if she really has hurt herself, which I doubt, then they're both going back to Nairobi. I've made up my mind.'

Tears were rolling down Afra's cheeks and splashing onto her knees. She tried not to sniff, not wanting Minette to know she was crying. Beside her, Minette's impatient foot was tapping on the sand, and when she spoke, Afra heard a sharp note in her voice.

'This is a little extreme, don't you think? It's their summer holiday, after all.'

'It's mine, too,' Prof said, almost petulantly. 'Yours and mine, in fact. And I'm not putting up with these stupid hysterics and tantrums any more.'

Silence fell.

'I'm surprised, Richard,' Minette said coolly. 'I

think that Afra's behaviour has been – understandable under the circumstances. She's a girl. Nearly a woman. She feels things very deeply.'

'She's impossible, rude, arrogant and selfish,' exploded Prof, 'and she's going back to Nairobi tomorrow. Then, perhaps, you and I can enjoy a little time together without being subjected to all this childish nonsense. Now don't, please, Minette, try to make me change my mind.'

'Oh, I won't.' Minette's voice hardened as she spoke. 'Clearly I haven't understood you very well. You're not quite the person I thought you were. I think it would be best if I went home to Nairobi too.' She stopped, as if waiting for Prof to say something, but he seemed too stunned to speak. 'I feel rather disappointed. The way you talked about Afra, I thought you really cared about her. I liked that in you.' She looked down at Afra. 'Don't let him bully you. I'm sorry I won't get to know you now. We could have been good friends.'

She turned, and began to walk quickly back along the beach in the direction of the hotel.

Afra sat still, aghast. The shock of Minette's departure had cleared her head of its dizziness. She stole a look at Prof. He looked dazed, as if he might be about to faint himself.

No one said anything. Afra waited for the surge of joy that would surely come upon her now that her enemy had gone, had fled the field, leaving her in triumphant possession of the prize, but the joy didn't come. Instead, she felt empty and almost disappointed.

Prof found his voice at last.

'I suppose you're satisfied now,' he said bitterly. 'You've got what you want.'

He began to walk away towards the guest house. Afra slumped down, her head on her knees again. Joseph ran after Prof.

'She can't walk, Prof,' he said. 'She really did get knocked out.'

Prof's shoulders had been stiff, but now they seemed to sag. He came back and looked down at Afra for a long minute.

'I'll get you back to bed,' he said, his voice flat. 'Have you really got concussion?' He sounded lifeless.

'I don't know. I don't know what concussion feels like.' She stole a glance at him. He seemed to have aged ten years in the last five minutes.

She struggled to her feet.

'It's OK. I can walk, I guess.'

Joseph had backed away from them again and was standing with his back to them, his shoulders hunched, looking out to sea. Prof followed her gaze.

'Joseph?' he said. His anger seemed to have gone. 'Are you coming?'

Joseph turned round and Afra saw, with a stab of guilt, that he was looking miserable. He didn't say much usually. He kept his feelings to himself, but she knew how much he'd been looking forward to this special holiday and how upset he would be at being sent home in disgrace.

He must be feeling just terrible, she thought, and I suppose it's all my fault.

Prof tried to put his hand under her arm to help her along, but she flinched away from him.

'I'm OK,' she said gruffly. 'I can manage.'

He bit his lip. She didn't know what to think. Perhaps he was sorry and wanted to make things up to her, but she wasn't sure she was ready for that. If he really was going to send her and Joseph back to Nairobi, he was being a hypocrite. She'd be angrier with him than ever.

She was feeling stronger now and managed the short walk back to the guest house without any help. She reached the door of her room and saw that Prof was watching her, his face blank.

'I'll bring you some tea,' he said. 'Go and lie down.'

Joseph had gone to his own room and shut his door. Afra stumbled to her bed and lay down on it. Her head was aching violently, and she felt very tired.

I just want it all to go away, she thought.

She found she had curled up like a baby. She reached under her pillow for her pyjamas, that were made of a soft, fluffy cotton, and cuddled them in her arms, like a teddy.

Prof opened her door a few minutes later, a mug of tea in his hand. He put it down on the table by her bed.

'Afra,' he began. She closed her eyes. She didn't think she could bear any more angry talk. 'It's OK. I won't send you home. You can stay here.'

He sounded detached, as if he didn't care about anything any more. She dared to look up at him. He was staring out of the window, as if he'd forgotten about her.

'Have you told Joseph?' she said, almost in a whisper. 'He was upset. It wasn't his fault, really, Prof. I made him come with me.'

He sighed heavily.

'I'll go and talk to him now.'

He went out and shut the door.

Tears trickled out of the corners of Afra's eyes and rolled past her ears onto the pillow. She felt suddenly cold, in spite of the heat of the day, and realized her clothes were still damp. Shakily, she sat up, slipped them off and put dry clothes on, then she wriggled under her blanket and lay on her back, looking unseeingly up at the ceiling, cradling the mug of hot tea in her hands.

Maybe I just ruined his life, she thought. Pictures crowded into her mind. She remembered the new youthfulness in Prof's face, which had disappeared the moment Minette had walked away. She remembered the new softness in him, a new kind of joy.

I killed all that, she told herself.

She finished her tea and looked at her watch. It had stopped. The glass was cracked and water had got in underneath it. She must have hit it when she'd fallen into the sea.

She had no idea what time it was. This miserable day seemed to have gone on forever. It was an eternity since breakfast, a lifetime since that awful moment when Hani had started digging near the turtle's nest, and she'd shouted at Minette.

She didn't want to think about it. Her eyes closed, and a moment later she was asleep.

When she woke up, she could see by the way the shadows were falling that it was late in the afternoon. Something had woken her. She lay puzzling over it for a moment, then realized that her door had been quietly shut. She sat up. Her head still ached but only a little, and the odd, rocking, dizzy sensation she'd felt before had gone.

She swung her legs over the side of the bed and felt for her shoes. She was nervous about seeing Prof and Joseph again, but there was no point in putting it off.

She stepped outside into the sunshine. Prof was sitting on a chair under a tree not five metres away. He had a book in his hands, but he wasn't reading it. He turned his head to look at her, and she was shocked by the misery in his face.

'Hi, honey,' he said, with a dismal attempt at a smile. 'How are you feeling? I just came to check on you. People with concussion aren't supposed to sleep too long, but you looked OK to me.'

'I am OK.' She didn't know how to respond. She could see he was trying to sound normal, but that he didn't feel normal at all. 'Where's Joseph?'

'He went to the village to see Hussein.' Her eyebrows shot up. 'It's OK. I said he could. We had a good talk. He knows I didn't mean half the things I said. I was – worried. It came out wrong. I—'

'It's all right,' she said quickly. 'You don't have to say anything.'

She wanted to run up to him, fling her arms round his neck and tell him she would never be moody and selfish and difficult again, that she'd only wanted them to be together, like they'd always been before, but she knew it wouldn't do any good. She would only wring a tired smile from him, and get a kindly pat on the head. Nothing she could do would make him feel any better.

She sat down beside him. An uncomfortable thought had occurred to her. There was something she could do. It would be surprising, difficult and possibly humiliating. But it was, amazingly, the thing she suddenly wanted to do most of all.

'I'm quite better now, Prof,' she said. 'I'm going for a little walk. No, it's OK. Don't come. I won't go far, I promise, and I'll be back soon.'

16

A CHANGE OF HEART

Afra went to her room and looked at herself anxiously in the mirror. Her T-shirt was clean, but that was all that could be said for it. She had nothing else, though, that looked any better.

She dragged a comb through her hair and put on her beach shoes. As she went to the door, her eye fell on her turtle poster and on an impulse she picked it up.

It seemed an unusually long way to the hotel and by the time she got there she was hot and her head was aching again. She walked up the path from the beach and skirted round the outside till she came to the hotel's main entrance at the front.

She stood for a moment, looking in through the double doors. The reception desk looked forbidding. An Indian couple, smartly dressed, with expensive suitcases on the floor beside them, were talking to a uniformed clerk, who was writing something down.

Afra waited. She felt uncomfortable, as out of place as a stray cat in this polished, perfumed, grandiose place.

The Indian couple moved away from the desk and a porter rushed forward to take their cases. The man behind the reception desk was free.

It's now or never, thought Afra, clutching her poster so tightly she was in danger of crushing it.

She stepped up to the desk.

'I want to see Miss—' she stopped. She didn't know Minette's surname! She wouldn't be able to ask for her! 'Her first name is Minette,' she finished lamely.

The reception clerk was tall and his dark face had snapped shut in a stern frown.

He thinks I'm a street child or a beggar or something, Afra thought, and she lifted her chin defiantly.

The man shook his head.

'There is no Minette here,' he said dismissively.

'Yes there is. She's staying here.' Afra was determined to stand her ground. 'She's a friend of my father, Professor Tovey.'

The word 'professor' had the desired effect. The man's expression altered slightly.

'Ah, you mean Miss Delarue,' he said. 'Yes, she was here. She checked out an hour ago.'

'Checked out?' The ground seemed to heave under Afra's feet. 'You mean she's gone already?'

'She's gone, yes,' the clerk said, losing interest.

'Where? Where did she go?'

The man shrugged.

'To the airport, perhaps. I don't know.'

Afra stood still, trying to absorb what he was saying. How could she have been so stupid? It was hours since Minette had told Prof she was going to leave. Of course she would have gone by now.

'How did she go?' she asked, feeling hopeless. 'Is there a bus from here? Or a taxi?'

'Taxi, bus, I don't know.' The clerk was losing patience. 'She's not here. Do you see the door? It's over there. The hotel is not open to non-residents. Goodbye.'

Afra felt insulted. Irritation gave her courage.

'Excuse me,' she said loudly. 'There's something else. I have – I made this poster. For the hotel. It's about turtles.' She faltered. The poster, which had looked so good in her room at the guest house, seemed to have shrunk. It looked crude and childish in contrast to the smartness of this hotel foyer.

The clerk looked at it disdainfully.

'The management does not permit advertising campaigns here. I told you. The door is over there. Go on.'

Afra drew a deep breath, prepared to argue, but the man's face was now so forbidding that she knew it would be useless. She breathed out again, on a heavy sigh, and turned away.

I'm useless, she thought. I wrecked Prof's life, probably, and I made everyone think I was just a stupid crazy kid, and I can't even draw a nice poster. I'm so pathetic.

Tears were welling up in her eyes and her throat was tight. She walked blindly towards the big double doors. She'd wait until she was outside, then she'd rip her poster to pieces and drop it into a litter bin.

Through the confused sounds of the hotel foyer, the murmur of voices, the swish of doors, the ping of the lift bell, she heard another noise – the patter of small clawed feet on the polished floor. A moment later, a sleek chestnut brown body was wriggling joyfully by her feet, and a little dachshund was whining hopefully as he looked up at her.

'Hani!' gasped Afra. 'What are you doing here? She can't have left you behind.'

She looked up. Minette had emerged from a side corridor and was standing beside a pillar a few metres away, looking at her with a wary, startled expression on her face.

Afra flushed. Now that the moment had come she had no idea what to say. She forced herself to walk up to Minette.

'I thought you'd gone,' she said.

'I have, nearly.' Minette looked at her watch. 'I'm waiting for my taxi.'

'Oh.' Afra cleared her throat. 'I brought my poster. The turtle one.' She remembered with painful clarity the moment when Prof and Joseph had admired the poster while Minette studied her unkind doodle. She flushed. 'They didn't want to pin it up here,' she went on, forcing herself to give a little laugh. 'I guess I don't blame them. I'm a real thicko at art. Always was. It never comes out right. I mean, when I draw something it's not what's in my head. It sort of looks different on the paper somehow. Do you know what I mean? If I want to draw a person, or something, it just comes out wrong. Weird, and . . .'

She knew she was talking nonsense but she didn't know how to stop.

'I thought you drew quite well,' Minette said drily. 'You seemed to express your feelings perfectly.'

Afra swallowed.

'No, no! I didn't! I sort of – well, that's really why I came. I thought if I saw you and talked to you—'

Minette looked surprised.

'You wanted to see *me*?'

'Yes!' Afra nodded enthusiastically. 'You see, I didn't, I mean, it wasn't—'

Minette seemed to come to a decision. She snapped her fingers to call Hani, who had chased off after a spider, and was ferreting behind a potted palm.

'Look,' she said briskly. 'We can't talk standing here. And you ought to be resting, after that bang on the head. Let's sit down over there, beside my bags.'

She led the way to a couple of armchairs set against the far wall of the foyer. They sat down. Minette looked at Afra, waiting for her to begin. Afra looked at her feet. She had no idea what to say.

'It's about your father, isn't it?' Minette said at last. She sounded sarcastic.

'Yes!' Afra burst out gratefully. 'He isn't horrible and cold, like you said. I would just hate for you to think that. It's only that he doesn't, well, he never tells you much what he's feeling. You have to kind of guess. To work it out, if you know what I mean. He's hardly ever, I mean, he's *never* really angry. It was because I was so horrible to you, and he wanted me to – well, he was embarrassed, you see, because he felt ashamed of me. I can see why he was. And he wanted you to like him. And to like me too, I suppose. But I didn't . . .'

Her voice tailed off.

'Why did you want to tell me all this?' Minette's voice was gentler now.

'Because he's so miserable!' Afra felt ready to cry again. 'I was shocked, I guess, when I met you first. He hadn't warned me or anything, and maybe I was jealous, or something. There was never anyone but Prof and me, you see, since my mother died. He really loved her. I thought he did, anyway. I thought he would stay, you know, kind of loyal to her.'

She wanted to add 'and to me', but the words didn't come out.

'Oh, he is loyal to her,' Minette said in an odd voice. 'Believe me, he is. I think he always will be.'

Afra looked at her, surprised, then shook her head vigorously, sending her dark curls flying.

'No. I thought about that this afternoon. I thought maybe it was me trying to make him feel those things. It wouldn't be fair of me if it was. She – my mother I mean – she died so long ago. Joseph said you can't expect someone to go on alone for ever, and I guess he's right. I thought I would be enough to make him happy, but I'm only his daughter. He said, Prof did, I mean, that he—' She couldn't stop her tears now and she didn't try. 'He said he guessed he ought to be allowed to see someone else after nearly thirteen years.'

Minette reached into one of her bags, pulled out a tissue and pushed it into Afra's hand. Afra took it gratefully, and blew her nose.

'*Ma pauvre*,' Minette said. 'You are an amazing girl, do you know that? Now I'm going to tell you how it really is. Your father is a very attractive man. Very fascinating.' Afra screwed the tissue into a tight ball and nodded cautiously, afraid of what might come. 'But,' Minette went on, 'he is not easy to get to know. I like him a lot. I thought I wanted to – to become close to him. But I'm not in love with him. Not at the moment, anyway. There's something that stops me, that blocks him.'

She seemed to be talking to herself. Afra listened with fascinated awe. It was the first time a grown-up had talked to her so confidentially. She felt as if she was grown-up too.

Minette was looking at her intently.

'I think that's why I decided to go. Not just because he was so nasty to you.'

'He didn't mean to be!' Afra said hastily. 'That's what I'm was trying to tell you. After you'd gone he was sorry. He wasn't angry any more. He's not sending us home or anything.'

Minette flashed her a brief smile.

'Good. I'm glad about that. But it wasn't only the way he treated you. It was the other thing, the feeling I have that he isn't free. That he still loves your mother. If I let myself fall in love with him, I would always be afraid of this – this unseen rival.'

Afra sat in silence, turning Minette's words over in her mind. She had wanted passionately to believe that Prof's love for her dead mother would be preserved intact for ever. Now she could see, if only dimly, that maybe it wasn't what she wanted after all. Maybe if Prof was released, to love someone else in a different way, there'd be more love to go around.

There might even be more for me, she thought. It might not be too bad. It might be kind of interesting.

Aloud, she said, 'I think you should give him another chance. I guess he could fall for you. You're really pretty. He's never been like this with anyone else, anyway.'

Minette made a funny choking noise. Afra was afraid she was trying not to laugh, then realized that she was trying not to cry.

'You love him, don't you?' she said.

Afra shrugged, and smiled shakily.

'I hate him sometimes. I hated you at first. I don't any more though. I don't even know you properly. I'm really sorry I said all those things and did that stupid drawing.'

Minette put an arm round Afra's shoulders and gave them a squeeze. Afra sat a little stiffly, breathing in Minette's perfume. She wasn't ready for embraces yet.

The clerk from the reception desk came up to them.

'Your taxi is here, madam,' he said.

Minette hesitated.

'She doesn't need it now,' said Afra, rushing her fences.

Minette stood up.

'No, I don't. And I would like my old room

back, please. I'm staying after all. Oh, and I wish to see the manager. I want to ask him about his turtle policy.'

'Turtle policy?' The clerk looked startled.

'Yes,' said Minette firmly. 'It's a disgrace. There is no awareness here, none at all. The first thing he needs to do is to make sure that this beautiful poster is displayed in a prominent position, where every guest is sure to see it.'

17

OUT TO SEA

It was only a short distance by road to the guest house, but Minette insisted on recalling the taxi and doing it in comfort. Secretly, Afra was relieved. Her head was still bad and her legs felt wobbly. It was an unfamiliar sensation to have someone kind and bossy, thinking about her comfort. Prof and Sarah, though she knew they loved her, usually left her to manage things on her own.

The rapid African twilight had already faded, and it was dark by the time they arrived back at the guest house. Prof was pacing up and down outside. He saw Afra climb out of the taxi and ran forward.

'Oh sweetheart, are you all right? I was so worried! I should never have let you—'

Then he saw Minette and stopped. Colour rushed into his face.

Minette was taking her time, getting money out of her purse to pay the taxi driver. She seemed reluctant to look up.

'It's OK, Prof,' Afra said. She was disappointed

to see that Prof's face had not immediately broken out into a happy smile. 'She's staying.'

Behind Prof she saw Joseph approaching from the shadowy garden. He was looking at her in disbelief. Afra felt embarrassed. She bent down to stroke Hani, fondling his silky ears.

Bending down made her feel a little dizzy. She longed to sink into one of the sagging old chairs on Mr Mohammed's veranda, and close her eyes, but Prof and Minette were still silent, looking awkwardly at each other, and she wanted to get out of the way.

'I can take Hani for a walk if you like,' she said uncertainly.

They both turned to her, as if glad of a diversion.

'Certainly not, honey, you've done too much today already,' Prof said. 'Sit here and rest. Minette and I will go down to the beach for a bit. We won't be long.'

Afra felt a spasm of regret and anxiety. Maybe it would always be like this now. Maybe Prof and Minette would always go off together, and leave her out of things. Then she saw that Minette was looking at her enquiringly, a pucker between her brows.

It's like she wants me to give her permission or something, she thought, surprised.

'OK,' she said. 'I'll see you guys later.'

She watched them go, then made it to the

veranda and sank down thankfully into a chair. Joseph sat down beside her.

'What happened?' he said. 'I thought she was going home?'

He looked mystified.

'It's kind of complicated,' she said, closing her eyes.

'Don't tell me then, if you don't want to.' He sounded huffy.

She opened her eyes again.

'Sorry. It's just that I'm feeling kind of weird. My head and everything. And I've been so crazy these last few days. I went to see Minette at the hotel. I told her I was sorry, and asked her to stay.'

'You asked her to stay?' Joseph looked thunderstruck. 'Why?'

'Oh, I don't know. I guess I had a few things to straighten out in my head. I didn't want to wreck Prof's life, for one thing. Anyway, I kind of like her. Sort of.'

'*What*?'

Afra stole a glance at him. He was shaking his head.

'I'm never going to understand girls,' he said. 'Not even if I live as long as my grandfather.'

Minette stayed for supper. It was an odd meal. She and Prof seemed almost shy with each other, and both of them treated Afra as if she was a guest of honour, plying her with the nicest bits of Mr Mohammed's delicious curries and choosing the best pieces of fruit for her from the dish. Joseph seemed too bemused to speak. He ate his way steadily through a large meal and surreptitiously tickled Hani's tummy under the table with his bare toes.

Afterwards, when the last mouthful had been eaten, and Mr Mohammed had brought in coffee for Prof and Minette, and settled down for a chat, Afra gave a mighty yawn.

'You must be exhausted, honey,' Prof said. 'Go to bed.'

'I will,' said Afra, surprising herself. She hadn't gone to bed so early for years.

'*Kwaheri*,' said Joseph, lapsing into Swahili.

'*Bonne nuit, ma petite*,' said Minette.

Back in her room, Afra sank into bed with a weariness so profound that her body seemed to melt into the sheet. She drifted away at once into sleep.

She was woken a few hours later by the sound of her door gently shutting. She turned over and peered out through the white film of her mosquito net, but her room was empty. Whoever had been there had gone.

Then she heard quiet voices outside.

'She's sleeping all right.' Prof's deep voice came in clearly through the open window.

'You should check on her again later.' Minette

was speaking now. 'After a head injury you have to be so careful.'

'I know.' Prof sounded worried. 'I should have kept her in bed this afternoon. I'm not much good at this kind of thing. Sarah always looks after her if she's sick. Sarah's been her mother, actually.'

'Yes. Afra was lucky.' Minette sounded thoughtful. 'But maybe she needs a little more help now than Sarah can give her.'

Afra turned onto her back. She caught her breath, ready to feel defensive if Sarah was insulted.

'Sarah still sees her as a child, maybe,' Minette went on, 'like mothers do, but Afra won't be a child much longer. You realize, Richard, don't you, that she's very beautiful?'

'Afra? Is she?' Prof sounded bewildered.

'Of course she is. Those huge eyes, and that lovely skin. Her face is unusually striking. Of course, her figure isn't mature yet, and she'll grow taller, but she's going to be extraordinary.'

'Oh.' Prof sounded more worried than pleased. 'Are you sure?'

Minette laughed. It was still a tinkly sound, but for some reason Afra found it more musical now. She pushed herself up on her pillow, feeling an odd sensation, half pleasure, half nervousness.

'She needs some decent clothes,' Minette went on. 'I couldn't bear to see what she had done to herself the other night.'

Afra bit her lip and felt herself reddening.

Thanks a lot, she thought angrily.

'She needs someone to do all those women's things with,' Minette was saying. 'She would look wonderful in strong colours – red, deep blue. You should get her hair cut properly. Bring out the shape of her head. Buy her some good jewellery.'

'She has her mother's cross,' said Prof. He sounded hunted. 'I don't know anything about that kind of thing.'

'Of course you don't, Richard.' Afra could hear that Minette was amused. 'Maybe she would let me take her shopping one day. It would be fun.'

Prof made a grunting noise.

'Oh, not yet,' Minette went on. 'She's not used to me. It takes time. I know what it's like for her. I had no mother either.'

They were moving off and their voices faded away.

Afra lay staring up into the net, jumbled thoughts and feelings churning round in her head.

She thinks I'm beautiful, she thought, blocking out the memory of her dreadfully made-up face. Red! I don't have any red clothes.

She rolled over. Sleep was overcoming her again. She was imagining herself in a scarlet dress and with an amazing new haircut, sweeping down a staircase towards a throng of admiring upturned faces. The idea was so strange it made her smile.

'I didn't know she never had a mother either,' she muttered. 'Prof should have told me.'

The next moment, she was deeply asleep.

Hours later, Joseph's hand on her shoulder woke her again. Early morning light was penetrating her room.

'Afra! Wake up!' Joseph whispered. 'Abel's here. One of the turtle nests hatched and Grace Otieno's going to check it to see if any of the babies are stuck and need help getting out. Do you want to come?'

She was awake at once.

'Give me a minute,' she said.

Joseph went outside while she scrambled hastily into her shorts. She picked up her white T-shirt and hesitated over it.

I do like red, she thought. And blue. Why didn't I think of it before?

Joseph was waiting impatiently for her.

'Is your head OK now?' he said.

She shook it experimentally.

'Sure. I don't feel a thing any more.'

They ran down to the beach. The nest was some way along towards the village, and they could see that Grace and Abel were standing beside it.

'Great. They haven't started yet,' said Afra, bounding towards them with the speed of a hare.

Grace beamed at them.

'I was going to come and see you later,' she said. 'I was at the hotel last night. The manager wanted to see me. He said some guests have been complaining about their turtle policy. "We don't have a turtle policy," he told me. "What are we going to do?" So I told him.'

'It was Minette,' Afra said. 'She laid into him. I couldn't believe it. She was great.'

Grace gave Afra a puzzled look and Afra looked down, embarrassed.

'How do you know the eggs have hatched?' said Joseph, stepping into the breach.

'Look here,' said Abel.

He pointed to a deep round hole at the side of the nest. Dry sand was already trickling down into it.

'A fisherman came to report it,' Grace said. 'He said that the hatching took place the night before last. He watched them. There were over a hundred, he thought. A good number. We have left it long enough. It's time to dig it out and rescue any stragglers.'

She nodded at Abel and he got down on his knees and began to scoop gently at the sand. Afra squatted down beside him. He was clearing a big area, sweeping the sand away with his hands like the mother turtle had done with her flippers.

Afra held her breath. What if they were wrong and the baby turtles hadn't hatched at all?

Digging them out like this might damage them, kill them even.

Abel was working up to his shoulder now, in the deep hole he had made. He grunted suddenly, and pulled his arm up. In his hand was a soft empty shell, a thick white membrane. He put into it Afra's hand. She felt it between her fingers. It was still a little moist, flexible and cool to the touch.

Abel was bringing up shell after empty shell now, laying them out on the sand so that Grace could count them. He paused, his arm deep in the hole, and then, very carefully, brought up a tiny living turtle.

'Put it down on the sand,' Grace said urgently. 'Let it go now.'

The little creature, its oval carapace no bigger than the palm of Afra's hands, raised its tiny beaked head. Then, as if it was responding to a call which nobody else could hear, it set off, its fragile, unpractised flippers flailing towards the sun which was rising over the sea.

Afra followed it with her eyes. The hatchling was going fast, and had reached a patch of seaweed.

'Can I carry him down to the sea?' she asked Grace.

Grace shook her head.

'No. He has to do this part himself. Something mysterious happens now. He is learning his own birthplace, his own beach. If he doesn't do this, you will cut his chances of survival. And he will not know where to return when the time comes for him to mate. Or if this little one is a female, she will not know where to come to make her nest.'

'Oh,' said Afra, watching the hatchling's struggle, her fingers itching to bend down and help.

But the hatchling was winning the struggle. With a forceful thrust it freed itself from the clinging seaweed and was off again, powering itself down the beach like a marathon runner racing for the tape.

Afra looked behind her. Abel had freed the last four baby turtles now, and they were streaming down the beach after the first one, leaving miniature tracks in the sand. Afra looked down towards the sea and shivered. A flock of white ghost crabs was scurrying about at the water's edge.

'Would the crabs go for the hatchlings?' she called back to Grace.

'Yes!' answered Grace. 'Drive them away.'

Afra raced down to the water. The crabs scattered in front of her. She went back to the struggling hatchling.

'Come on,' she murmured, mentally urging it on. 'It's safe for you now.'

The hatchling had stopped, as if resting for a moment, then he was off again, racing across the vast desert of sand. He had made it to the firmer damper sand, an easier surface for him to manage, and he was going fast. The smell of the sea was in his nostrils.

His siblings had caught him up. Stronger than him, their flippers were flailing diligently, covering the metres, leaving him behind. Theirs was the advantage in this race for life, in this desperate struggle.

Afra watched, her heart in her mouth.

What if he doesn't make it? she thought. What if he just gives up? I'll have to help him then.

They were nearly at the water's edge now. A wave reached out for the hatchling, then cruelly receded, leaving him floundering in the sodden sand. Another, kindlier ripple came for him, and picked him up in its welcoming arms. The hatchling found his form. The paddling movements that had been so hard on land served him well now, and with a powerful kick he was through the first wave. Another rolled him over, and for a moment Afra was afraid that he would never make it, would never thrust his way past the breakers to the greater safety of the deeper ocean.

'Go on! You can do it!' breathed Afra. She wanted to plunge into the water after him, to pick him up and carry him out to the reef, where there would be plants for him to feed on, and safe havens in the crevices where he could hide from the many predators that were lying in wait in these shallow waters.

But I can't, she told him silently. You have to do this alone.

The hatchling survived the buffeting of the next wave and disappeared out of Afra's sight. She stood, thigh deep in water, peering at the surface of the waves. Twice she saw a little head, no bigger than the tip of her thumb, as the hatchling came up for air, and then he was gone.

She watched for a long time, seeing the white crests of the waves breaking far out on the reef ahead. Terror lay out there, and pleasure, food, rest, sleep and play. And one day, if the little turtle lived, he might come home to find a mate, and she would make a nest, and lay more eggs, to hatch in their turn in the soft sand.

'You've just got to grow up, baby,' whispered Afra. 'You're on your own now.'

She turned and splashed out of the sea, towards the breakfast that waited for her in the guest house.

Elizabeth Laird
Wild Things 4:
RHINO FIRE

It is the rhino's only chance of survival . . .

As the animal charges away from the speeding helicopter, Titus leans perilously out to take aim with his long dart gun. If only the rare black rhino can be relocated to a new reserve, Afra and Joseph know it might join the few others of its kind.

But at Nakuru the rhino faces a far greater danger. Men armed with powerful rifles, who will kill it for its valuable horn. And who are ready to shoot any child that tries to stop them . . .

Elizabeth Laird

Wild Things 5:
RED WOLF

The wolf's coat was a vivid russet colour, luxuriously thick. His deep amber eyes looked fearlessly into Afra's.

On a desolate mountain plateau, Afra comes face to face with one of the rarest animals in the world – the Ethiopian wolf. The survival of this beautiful creature somehow seems deeply connected with her quest to find out if her long-lost family is alive. Her desperation to save the wolves makes her take a terrible risk to protect a den of pups. A risk that puts Afra herself in serious danger . . .

Elizabeth Laird
Wild Things 6:
ZEBRA STORM

The Grevy zebra is unmistakable. It is the most beautiful of its kind. But there are very few of them left in Africa.

Joseph, Afra and Tom are lucky to find a magnificent Grevy stallion at a remote water hole. But it is alone and wounded, and a prowling lion is on its trail. Joseph is especially determined to save it. Like the zebra, he's in a desperate state. He's just been reunited with a man he's hated all his life – his father. Scared and angry, he runs away into the bush – straight into the lion's hungry jaws . . .

Elizabeth Laird
Wild Things 7:
PARROT RESCUE

The parrot seemed to be thinking. He flashed his brilliant flame-coloured tail feathers.
'Wanna nut,' he said.

Tom and Afra are having a great time looking after an amazing African Grey parrot. But they know that thousands of these birds die in the cruel trade that smuggles wild parrots out of Africa. Then Tom boards a flight from Nairobi to England and notices a man carrying a suspicious package. All alone, at London's vast airport terminal, Tom knows he must act fast – and sets off on a reckless and dangerous chase . . .